BACKROADS BLOOD BROTHERS

BACKROADS BLOOD BROTHERS

W. DALE JORDAN

ONE

THE FIRST STEP IS TO MAKE SURE THEY THINK IT'S THEIR IDEA.

IT'S SURPRISINGLY EASY.

YES, BUT IT HAS TO BE THEIR IDEA.

OF COURSE, WE TEASE THEM.

NATURALLY.

THE TEASING IS HONESTLY MY FAVORITE PART.

NO, IT ISN'T.

OKAY, NO, IT ISN'T. NOT REALLY ... THAT PART COMES LATER.

WE ARE NATURALLY SEDUCTIVE. SOMETHING ABOUT THE COMBINATION OF OUR DARK, BLACK HAIR AND GREEN EYES.

IT'S MAGNETIC.

INTENSE.

BARS ARE THE EASIEST.

CLUBS ARE TOO NOISY.

PEOPLE TRAVEL IN PACKS.

YOU'LL ALMOST ALWAYS FIND SOMEONE LONELY —

HORNY ....

— THAT, TOO, IN A BAR.

"Are you twins?"

IT'S THE DUMBEST QUESTION. WE ARE, WITHOUT QUESTION, IDENTICAL, BUT YOU'D BE SURPRISED HOW MANY PEOPLE LEAD WITH THAT. WE GRIN SHEEPISHLY AT ONE ANOTHER.

WE'VE PRACTICED THIS IN THE MIRROR FOR YEARS TO ENSURE IT'S EXACTLY RIGHT. OUR LIPS CURL AT JUST THE RIGHT ANGLE. WE SHOW THE SAME NUMBER OF TEETH. WE BOTH LOOK AWAY FROM ONE ANOTHER. IT EMBARRASSES THEM, BUT IT ALSO INTRIGUES THEM.

WITH MOST, YOU CAN ALMOST SEE WHEN THEY START FANTASIZING.

"YEAH, WE'RE TWINS. I'M CALEB."

"AND I'M CONNOR. WHAT'S YOUR NAME?"

"Mark," he says.

IT'S A BIT ON THE NOSE, BUT NOT SO MUCH THAT IT MAKES THINGS LESS INTERESTING. I TURN ON MY BARSTOOL TO FACE HIM. I AM SITTING BETWEEN HIM AND CALEB. THIS IS IMPORTANT. YOU WANT HIM TO LEAN IN A BIT TO MAKE SURE HE'S SEEING WHAT HE THINKS HE SEES.

MARK LOOKS LIKE HE MIGHT BE AROUND FORTY OR SO, AT LEAST TEN YEARS OLDER THAN US, BUT IT MIGHT JUST BE THAT HE'S HAD A HARDER TIME THAN WE HAVE. STILL, HE'S GOOD-LOOKING IN THAT ROUGHNECK KIND OF WAY THAT WE LIKE. SANDY BLOND HAIR AND BLUE EYES IN A CHISELED FACE WITH JUST THE RIGHT AMOUNT OF STUBBLE. WE SAW HIM AS SOON AS WE CAME INTO THE BAR.

HE'S WEARING A TIGHT GREY MUSCLE SHIRT THAT SHOWS OFF HIS LEAN BUILD. TONED SHOULDERS AND BICEPS LEAD DOWN TO VEINY FOREARMS, AND CALLOUSED HANDS WRAPPED LOOSELY AROUND HIS BEER GLASS. THE LIGHTEST DUSTING OF BLONDE CHEST HAIR PEEKS FROM THE TOP OF HIS SHIRT. HE'S FUCKING GORGEOUS.

"I GOTTA TAKE A LEAK," I SAY, OR, SOMETIMES, "WE NEED BETTER MUSIC."

WHATEVER IT IS, I'LL STEP AWAY FOR A FEW MINUTES AND LET CONNOR START WORKING ON HIM.

"WE'RE NOT, ACTUALLY. TOTALLY IDENTICAL, I MEAN."

"Oh?" he asks, sipping cheap beer.

"Yeah, we're actually mirror twins."

"What's that?"

"Basically, it means we're identical, but opposite. Like, I have a heart-shaped birthmark on my right pec. He has the same, but it's on the left. I'm right-handed, and he's left-handed. I have a little mole in the crease of my thigh right next to my dick. He has the same on the left. Everything else is pretty much *exactly* the same."

"Oh," he says, looking mildly uncomfortable. He looks directly at his beer, but I see his eyes move in my direction, down toward my crotch. I've almost set the hook.

"Your beer's almost empty," I say, returning from whatever made-up thing I went to do. This time I stand on the opposite side of Mark, fencing him in between us.

"Yeah," he says.

"You want another?"

"Uh ... sure."

"Hey, barkeep, can we get another round over here?" We don't drink, but it's important to look like we do.

"I was just explaining to Mark that we're not totally identical."

"It's true. I think the latest stats say that mirror twins make up about twenty-five percent of all identical twins."

"So, as a pair, we're one in four, but we like to think we're more special than that."

We let the conversation go quiet as the bartender brings our drinks over. Mark tries to pay, but I won't let him. We pay in cash only. No credit cards, no paper trails, no nothing. It's hard enough doing this as twins. We stand out in a crowd.

For our looks as much as the fact that we're twins.

It's a curse.

"So, Mark, what are you doing out tonight?"

"It's been a long week. Just wanted to have a drink."

"That's cool, but why don't you have a date?"

"Yeah, is there a Mrs. Mark somewhere?"

"No," he says.

We smile at him.

"What's wrong with the women around here? Don't they know a good thing when they see it?"

"Had a girlfriend, but she moved out a couple of weeks ago."

Bingo!

Perfect!

"That sucks, man. What happen? She meet someone new?"

His body tenses. I struck a nerve.

"No," he lies and takes a long pull from his beer glass.

Poor guy.

"Caleb, what's wrong with you? Sorry about that. He's nosey."

Mark stares at his beer but shrugs.

Caleb looks at me and nods. So close.

"My best friend," he mumbles.

"What?"

"She was fucking my best friend."

What is this? A country song?

"That's fucked up!"

"Tell me about it," he mumbles again.

"YEAH, MAN, I'M SORRY. YOU WANT ANOTHER BEER?"

HE LOOKS AT ME, REALLY LOOKS AT ME, THEN TURNS AND LOOKS AT CALEB.

THOSE BLUE EYES. I THINK HE'S PUT TWO AND TWO TOGETHER. WE'RE ABOUT TO HAVE TO FIGHT OUR WAY OUT OF THIS BAR, OR WE'RE GOING TO GET WHAT WE CAME FOR WITHOUT BREAKING A SWEAT.

"I DON'T MIND BUYING ANOTHER ROUND," I TELL HIM.

"I gotta piss," he says, pushing away from the bar. He half stumbles as he stands, more from the swiveling stool than beer.

"YEAH, MAN, NO PROBLEM," I TELL HIM. "WE'LL BE HERE IF YOU WANT ANOTHER ROUND OR ... SOMETHING."

I LEAN AGAINST THE BAR FACING OUT. CONNOR IS TURNED AROUND, FACING THE BARTENDER. WHEN MARK GETS TO THE BATHROOM DOOR, HE TURNS, LOOKS BACK AT ME FOR A SECOND, THEN GIVES AN ALMOST IMPERCEPTIBLE NOD TOWARD THE DOOR BEFORE ENTERING.

"HOOKED HIM," I SAY, PUSHING FROM THE BAR AND WALKING AFTER HIM.

I WAIT. THIS IS WHERE WE REEL THEM IN, BUT WE CAN'T GO IN THERE TOGETHER. WE CAN'T REALLY DO WHAT WE WANT HERE.

TOO MANY PEOPLE AROUND. ALL WE NEED IS SOME REDNECK TO WALK IN WHILE WE'RE IN THE MIDDLE OF A FUCK-CHAIN. WORLD WAR III IN A BAR TOILET? NO THANKS. I SIGH AND DRINK MY BEER.

HE'S STANDING AT THE URINAL WHEN I WALK INTO THE RESTROOM. THE WAY HE STANDS. I KNOW HE WAS WAITING FOR ME. I ALSO KNOW HE'S NOT ENTIRELY SURE WHY. I STAND AT THE DOOR FOR A FEW SECONDS, WATCHING HIM WATCH ME OVER HIS SHOULDER. I LIFT AN EYEBROW AND GRIN AT HIM.

"YOU EVER BEEN WITH A MAN BEFORE?"

He looks back at the wall. "No."

"BUT YOU'VE THOUGHT ABOUT IT."

"I – maybe."

"THAT'S COOL."

I WALK CLOSER TO HIM. "NOTHING WRONG WITH A LITTLE EXPERIMENTATION. RIGHT?"
I SLIP MY ARMS AROUND HIM FROM BEHIND, CAREFUL NOT TO LET OUR BODIES COMPLETELY TOUCH. THE BOND IS TENUOUS AT THIS POINT. TOO MUCH, TOO QUICKLY, AND WE'D LOSE HIM.

"No. I guess."

I SLIP MY HAND UNDER THE HEM AT THE BOTTOM OF HIS SHIRT AND SLIDE IT FORWARD. HIS ABS ARE DEFINED, NOT FROM WEIGHTLIFTING, BUT FROM WORK. YOU CAN TELL THE

DIFFERENCE. THERE'S SOMETHING MORE NATURAL ABOUT MUSCULATURE EARNED UNDER THE HOT TEXAS SUN. IT'S LESS PRETENTIOUS THAN THE SCULPTING THAT GOES ON IN AIR-CONDITIONED GYMS WITH SAUNAS AND SHOWERS. I ALSO NOTE THAT THE DUSTING OF HAIR ON HIS CHEST TRAVELS DOWN. MY PINKY CAN JUST BARELY FEEL THE COARSE HAIR THAT GROWS UP FROM THE BASE OF HIS COCK. NATURAL.

JUST LIKE WE LIKE IT.

I LEAN FORWARD JUST ENOUGH SO THAT I KNOW HE'LL FEEL MY BREATH ON THE BACK OF HIS NECK.

"YOU COULD HAVE US BOTH IF YOU WANTED. WE LIKE YOU." HIS BODY TENSES AGAIN, BUT THIS TIME IT'S DIFFERENT. THIS TIME, THERE'S A HEAT ON HIS SKIN, A FLUSH TO THE TAN THAT SPEAKS TO SOMETHING DEEPER. THE LOWEST MOAN ESCAPES HIS THROAT. HE SWALLOWS HARD AND LEANS BACK SLIGHTLY UNTIL HIS BACK PRESSES AGAINST MY CHEST.

I WATCH THEM EMERGE FROM THE BATHROOM. MARK DOESN'T LOOK AT ME. HE HEADS STRAIGHT FOR THE DOOR. CALEB SMILES AND NODS. WE'RE IN BUSINESS. I'VE ALREADY PAID OUR TAB. WE MEET IN THE MIDDLE OF THE BAR, A SILENT COMMUNICATION PASSING BETWEEN US. THERE'S NO NEED FOR WORDS NOW. WE GOT WHAT WE CAME FOR. THE BAR PATRONS IGNORE US AS WE WALK OUT THE DOOR. PEOPLE ONLY REALLY SEE WHAT THEY WANT, AND IN A BAR LIKE THIS, THEY'RE FAR MORE CONCERNED WITH THEIR BEER AND POOL THAN A SET OF TWINS THEY'VE NEVER SEEN BEFORE AND WILL NEVER SEE AGAIN.

MARK IS JUST GETTING INTO HIS TRUCK AS WE STEP OUT INTO THE NIGHT. HE STARTS HIS ENGINE BUT WAITS UNTIL WE'VE SETTLED INTO OUR OWN CAR BEFORE HE BACKS OUT OF HIS SPACE AND PULLS OUT ONTO THE LONELY ROAD. WE FOLLOW AT A SAFE DISTANCE. WHEN HE TURNS, WE TURN. WHEN HE STOPS, WE STOP.

HE PAUSES AS HE PASSES A STOP SIGN. WE OBEY THE LAW. STOP, LOOK BOTH WAYS, THEN FOLLOW HIM UNTIL HE PULLS ONTO A DARK DIRT ROAD THAT DOUBLES AS HIS DRIVEWAY LEADING UP TO HIS HOUSE.

HE DOESN'T SPEAK WHEN HE EXITS THE TRUCK. HE DOESN'T EVEN LOOK BACK AT US. WE FOLLOW HIM ONTO A PORCH LIT BY A SINGLE LIGHT AS LONELY AS HE IS. HE DOESN'T TURN ON THE LIGHTS IN THE ROOM WE ENTER. WE HOLD HANDS AND FOLLOW HIS FOOTSTEPS INTO THE DARKNESS. HIS BEDROOM IS AT THE BACK OF THE HOUSE. ONLY HERE DOES HE TURN ON A SINGLE LAMP. ITS GLOOMY LIGHT CASTS SHADOWS AROUND THE ROOM. I CAN FEEL CONNOR'S PULSE IN HIS FINGERS. I KNOW HIS COCK IS HARDENING JUST LIKE MINE IS.

IT TAKES A MOMENT FOR MARK TO TURN AND FACE US. HE LOOKS FROM ME TO CONNOR AND BACK AGAIN.

"Can I see?" he asks.

WE SMILE.

IT'S ANOTHER PERFORMANCE, BUT ONE WE KNOW WELL. WE REMOVE OUR SHIRTS FIRST AND WATCH MARK LOOK FROM

ONE CHEST TO THE OTHER. HE TAKES NOTE OF THE MIRRORED
BIRTHMARKS AND LICKS HIS LIPS AT THE SIGHT. WE STEP CLOSER
TO EACH OTHER AND WRAP OUR ARMS AROUND EACH OTHER'S
WAIST.

OUR HIPS ARE SLIM, OUR TORSOS TONED. OUR BROWN SUGAR
NIPPLES STAND OUT AGAINST PALE SKIN. WE HAVE THE SMALLEST
PATCH OF HAIR BETWEEN OUR PECS. WE KNOW THE EFFECT WE
HAVE ON OUR ADMIRERS.

"WILL YOU?"

HE LOOKS DOWN, AND WE LOOK AT EACH OTHER, SMILING,
BEFORE WE PUSH OFF OUR SHOES, UNFASTEN OUR BELTS,
UNBUTTON OUR FLIES, AND SLIP OUR PANTS DOWN AND OFF, ONCE
AGAIN RETURNING TO A STANDING POSITION. HE STARES DOWN
AT OUR TRIMMED PUBIC HAIR, AND I CAN SEE HIM LOOKING FOR
THE MOLES I TOLD HIM ABOUT.

"You guys really do this together?"

"YES."

"Why?"

"WHY NOT? WE'RE AS CLOSE AS ANY TWO PEOPLE CAN BE.
WE REALIZED WHAT WE BOTH LIKED AT THIRTEEN, AND EVERY
SO OFTEN, WHEN THE MOOD IS RIGHT, WE GO LOOKING FOR
SOMEONE TO SHARE THAT WITH. WHAT COULD BE MORE
NATURAL?"

"IT'S LIKE SEEING YOURSELF IN THE MIRROR. THE ONLY DIFFERENCE IS, WE CAN TOUCH OUR REFLECTION."

AS I SAY IT, I SLIDE THE BACK OF MY HAND DOWN MY BROTHER'S TORSO, OVER HIS SMOOTH STOMACH, AND DOWN TO HIS COCK, WHICH IS SO LIKE MINE THAT IT FEELS LIKE MASTURBATION WHEN I BEGIN TO STROKE HIM. CALEB RETURNS THE FAVOR. A SHEEN OF SWEAT BREAKS OUT OVER MARK'S FACE.

"IT MUST BE LONELY OUT HERE."

"NO ONE AROUND FOR MILES."

"In a small town like this, everyone knows your business."

"THEY KNOW WHAT SHE DID TO YOU."

"KNOW HOW SHE HUMILIATED YOU."

"LEFT YOU FOR A MAN WHO WAS SUPPOSED TO BE YOUR BEST FRIEND."

"I CAN'T IMAGINE WHAT THAT DOES TO YOU."

"BUT EVEN A MAN NEEDS TO FEEL WANTED."

"AND WE WANT YOU, MARK. WE WANT YOU LIKE YOU'LL NEVER BE WANTED AGAIN."

"THAT COUNTS FOR SOMETHING, RIGHT? EVEN IF IT'S SOMETHING YOU'VE NEVER DONE BEFORE?"

WE'RE FULLY ERECT. I CAN FEEL THE SLICK OF PRECUM SURROUND THE HEAD OF MY COCK. CALEB KNOWS EXACTLY HOW I LIKE IT.

CONNOR KNOWS PRECISELY HOW MUCH PRESSURE TO APPLY.

I HEAR HIS BREATH CATCH IN HIS THROAT. MY OWN MIRRORS HIS. I FEEL OUR HEARTBEATS COMPLETELY SYNC BY THE PULSE IN OUR COCKS.

MARK SLIPS HIS SHIRT UP AND OFF. IT'S EXACTLY AS I HAD IMAGINED IT. WE LICK OUR LIPS IN RESPONSE.

WHEN HE SLIPS HIS PANTS DOWN, I MOAN. HE'S THICK, EXACTLY LIKE I LIKE THEM. CONNOR LOOKS AT ME AND NODS, AND WITHOUT A WORD, I LIE DOWN ON THE BED, PUSHING MYSELF BACK TO GIVE MARK ROOM. I REACH OUT A HAND TO HIM, AND AFTER A MOMENT, HE TAKES IT. HE CLIPS ONTO HIS KNEES ON THE BED AND BENDS DOWN TO KISS MY STOMACH. HIS LIPS ARE SURPRISINGLY SOFT, BUT HIS HANDS ARE AS ROUGH AS I IMAGINED. HE SLIPS THEM UP MY SIDES, KISSING UP MY CHEST TO TEASE ONE OF MY NIPPLES WITH HIS MOUTH.

I GASP AND PUSH BACK ONTO THE BED. HE SUCKS AND NIBBLES HARDER IN RESPONSE. AFTER A MOMENT, I RUN MY FINGERS INTO HIS HAIR AND PULL HIS MOUTH UP TO MINE. HE STARTS TO PULL AWAY, BUT I HOLD HIM, LOOKING INTO HIS EYES.

"PLEASE," I WHISPER. "PLEASE."

HE HOLDS OUT FOR ANOTHER MOMENT BEFORE CAVING, BENDING

DOWN TO KISS MY LIPS. IT'S TENUOUS, LIKE A BUTTERFLY'S WINGS ON A ROSE PETAL IN THE BEGINNING. HE TASTES OF BEER AND CIGARETTE SMOKE. I FLICK MY TONGUE OVER HIS LIPS UNTIL HE OPENS THEM TO ME.

I WATCH THEM FOR A MOMENT, ADMIRING THE ECSTASY ON MY BROTHER'S FACE, BEFORE I SLIDE A HAND UP MARK'S SPINE AND ONTO HIS SHOULDERS, THEN TRACE MY FINGERS BACK DOWN TO HIS ASS AND BETWEEN HIS LEGS TO HIS EXPOSED COCK. HE'S ALREADY SLICKED UP. HE SHUDDERS AS I SWIVEL MY PALM AROUND AND AROUND THE TIP.

"YOU WANT TO FUCK HIM?"

HE HEARS MY WHISPER AND GRUNTS. I TAKE THAT AS A YES AND RETRIEVE A SMALL BOTTLE OF LUBE I KEEP IN MY POCKET FOR JUST SUCH AN OCCASION. HE CONTINUES TO KISS CALEB AS I MASSAGE IT INTO MY BROTHER'S ASS. HE, TOO, GRUNTS. I KNOW EXACTLY HOW MUCH HE LIKES IT. I POUR MORE INTO MY HAND AND SLIP IT AROUND MARK'S COCK, GETTING HIM LUBED UP JUST ENOUGH. CALEB BREAKS THE KISS AND BEGINS TO WIGGLE BACK MORE ONTO THE BED. MARK FOLLOWS HIM.

CALEB PUTS HIS LEGS UP ONTO MARK'S SHOULDERS, AND WITH A BIT OF HELP FROM ME, OUR LOVER SLIDES SLOWLY AND CAREFULLY INTO MY TWIN.

MY EYES ROLL BACK IN MY HEAD. GOD, HE FEELS GOOD. HE TAKES HIS TIME, FEELING ME OUT. HE PRESSES FORWARD A LITTLE HARDER, AND I MOAN TO LET HIM KNOW HE'S DOING IT RIGHT. I

SLIP MY HANDS DOWN HIS BACK, READJUSTING SO I CAN GRAB HIS ASS. I PULL HIM FORWARD HARDER INTO ME, AND HE FOLLOWS MY LEAD. CONNOR STARES AT ME FROM OVER MARK'S SHOULDER. SWEAT BEADS ON HIS FOREHEAD. HIS BREATH IS QUICK. I KNOW HE WON'T BE ABLE TO WAIT MUCH LONGER.

HE DIPS DOWN BESIDE THE BED AND REEMERGES IN A SWIFT MOTION.

"What are you doing?" Mark asks.

"SSSHH, JUST RELAX."

HE MOANS AS I CONTINUE. HE KNOWS WHAT'S COMING, BUT HE'S SO DEEP INTO CALEB THAT HE'S NOT FIGHTING IT. THE BED CREAKS WHEN I CLIMB ONTO IT. I LOOK DOWN AT MY TWIN, AND HE NODS AGAIN, PUTTING HIS HANDS ON MARK'S ASS, PULLING THE CHEEKS APART FOR ME. MARK GRUNTS WHEN I FIRST PUSH INTO HIM. I DON'T BLAME HIM. THIS IS DEFINITELY THE GUY'S FIRST TIME. HE'S SO TIGHT EVEN AFTER MY MASSAGING.

HE SLOWS HIS PACE. HE WOULD STOP COMPLETELY, EXCEPT THAT HE'S FAR TOO INVESTED NOW. HIS BODY'S AUTOPILOT HAS TAKEN OVER. WE ARE RIDING TOWARD THE INEVITABILITY OF ORGASM. I MOVE MY HIPS SLOWLY, BACK AND FORTH, IN AND OUT, UNTIL MARK RELAXES AGAIN, HIS OWN HIPS FALLING INTO MY RHYTHM.

THERE'S A MOMENT WHEN WE DO THIS, EVERY TIME WHEN I'M ALMOST POSITIVE I CAN FEEL CONNOR INSIDE ME. IT'S AS THOUGH HE REACHES THROUGH MARK'S BODY TO TOUCH ME ALSO. CONNECTED IN A WAY THAT WE HAVEN'T BEEN SINCE THE WOMB.

CLOSER THAN ANY TWO PEOPLE CAN BE.

I MOVE FASTER.

MARK MOVES FASTER.

I BITE HIS BACK. HE ASKS FOR MORE.

"FUCK ME, MARK."

"Fuck," he moans.

I CAN FEEL HIS INSIDES CONSTRICTING. IT DOESN'T TAKE LONG THE FIRST TIME A MAN IS FUCKED. HE'S RUNNING FOR THE PRECIPICE AT BREAKNECK SPEED NOW.

PLEASURE VERGES ON PAIN.

PAIN THAT BRINGS PLEASURE.

I LOOK INTO CONNOR'S EYES.

CALEB TOUCHES THE HEART-SHAPED BIRTHMARK ON HIS CHEST THAT MIRRORS MY OWN. I SWEAR I FEEL HIM TOUCHING MINE. IT BURNS.

I ARCH MY BACK. MARK'S GROANS BECOME SOMETHING MORE.

FRENZIED.

PRIMAL.

HE WANTS THIS, BUT HE ALSO NEEDS IT.

I NOD AT CALEB.

I DRAW THE RAZOR ACROSS MARK'S NECK.

THE WORLD BECOMES CRIMSON.
HIS BODY CONVULSES AND TIGHTENS AROUND ME.

WARM AND WET.

I WRAP MY ARMS AROUND MARK'S CHEST AS I FILL HIM.

I SPILL ONTO MY STOMACH, RUNNING MY HANDS THROUGH IT,
MIXING IT WITH BLOOD. EVERY NERVE ON FIRE.

I SIGH.

I SMILE.

"IT'S BEEN TOO LONG."

"YES."

I SLIP OUT OF MARK AS MY BREATHING RETURNS TO NORMAL. MY HEART
STILL POUNDS IN MY CHEST. IT WILL GO ON FOR A WHILE. I WRAP AN
ARM AROUND HIS WAIST AND GENTLY REMOVE HIM FROM CALEB.

I HATE THE EMPTINESS AFTER. I HOLD OUT MY ARMS TO CONNOR
AFTER HE DROPS MARK'S NAKED BODY ONTO THE FLOOR.

I GO TO HIM. WRAP MY ARMS AROUND HIM. BLOOD AND SEMEN MIX TOGETHER ON MY CHEST.

I PULL CALEB CLOSE.

THIS IS ACTUALLY MY FAVORITE PART.

YES, IT IS. ARMS AROUND EACH OTHER'S WAIST.

FOREHEAD TO FOREHEAD.

COCK TO COCK.

HEARTBEATS IN SYNC.

TOGETHER. JUST LIKE IN THE WOMB.

MY MIRROR.

AND MINE.

Two

LANE THREW HIS truck in neutral and was out the door before it had come to a complete stop. He was sick of Mark's shit. Yeah, he'd done a shitty thing, but he was man enough to admit it. He hadn't meant to fall in love with Jessica, but it happened. Still, he missed his best friend, and they were going to talk if he had to knock Mark's lights out to get it done.

His friend's house was quiet as he approached. The front door was open, and through the screen door, he could see all the lights were turned out. Lane stopped briefly, craning his neck to reassure himself that he'd seen Mark's truck in the drive as he approached. It was there, right where he always parked it.

So why did he suddenly feel like something was wrong?

He frowned and stepped up to the door, peeking inside.

"Mark? You in there?"

He waited, listening intently for some sign that he'd been heard.

"Mark, god damn it, answer me."

He paced in front of the door. In his mind, Mark was sitting in the dark looking at him, probably ready to swing if he came inside. That'd be about right.

When they were kids, Lane had thrown Mark under the bus when one of their teachers accused them of cheating. The truth was Lane had cheated. He'd begged Mark to let him copy his homework, and both had been too stupid to realize they'd get caught if they had the exact same answers on everything.

Their teacher cornered Lane first, and he cracked like an egg. Only the way he told it, Mark was the one who hadn't done the work. Mark was the one who had copied.

The teacher believed his crocodile tears, and Mark got detention for a week.

They didn't speak until the week ended, and Lane was sure he'd lost his best friend. When he couldn't take it anymore, he walked over to Mark's house, bypassing the front door, and went straight back to the shed where they played. The shed was dark when he first peeked inside. He was just about to turn back to the house when a fist came out of nowhere. Mark knocked his lights out and then stood over him, breathing hard.

"Were you waiting in there just in case I came over?" he'd asked.

"I knew you would eventually, asshole."

They instinctively looked toward the house to ensure Mark's mother hadn't heard him curse.

"I'm sorry," Lane said.

"I know. Now apologize."

They stared each other down for another minute before Lane's face broke into a smile. After a pause, Mark did the same. Within an hour, it was like it had never happened. Over the years, a lot of squabbles had been finished this way. It was like an unwritten rule. You had one punch. You put all your fucked up feelings into it and let it go.

It almost always worked.

"Fuck it," Lane muttered. "I'm coming in, Mark. One and done, and then we're gonna fucking talk. Right?"

Mark didn't answer, and Lane didn't wait.

He was through the door and into the house in three steps. His body naturally tensed, expecting the sucker punch he deserved. When it didn't come, he looked around. Nothing was turned on in the house. The lights were out. The TV was off. Worst of all, the coffeemaker sat quiet and empty.

That was *not* good.

"Mark?"

He crept toward his best friend's bedroom, sure that he would find him passed out drunk in bed. "Mark? Buddy?" He reached for the light switch, flipped it on, and turned toward the bed. "Are you –"

Lane fell back against the wall, covering his mouth and nose. He stumbled away from Mark's body, lying on the floor in a pool of blood. Ants and flies were already making themselves at home on the corpse, and he retched as a fat housefly crawled across his friend's open eye.

He turned away from the body and crawled toward the front door. The sunlight beyond the screen door was so distant he thought he'd never reach it, but he did, and as he pushed himself over the threshold, he heaved, vomiting his breakfast onto the steps.

Coughing and sputtering, he managed to avoid putting his hands into the vomit, rolling away from it onto his back, where he fumbled in his jeans pocket for his phone. Still shaking, he dialed the police station.

"Sheriff's department."

The answering voice was bored, but he knew the owner right away.

"Ashley?"

"Who is this?"

"Ashley, this is Lane. Mickey's brother?"

"Lane, why the hell are you calling the sheriff's office?"

"Ashley, Mark Haskell's dead."

"*What?!*"

"I'm at his house. Someone murdered him."

"Lane, that's not funny."

"Do I sound like I'm fucking joking?!"

"Oh my god," Ashley said, suddenly all business. "You sit your ass down and don't move. Someone's on the way."

Someone turned out to be Sheriff Jace Winters and his number one deputy, Kara Thoms. They took their time getting out of their patrol cars. Kara's hand rested on her sidearm, but Jace just shook his head.

"If this is a joke –"

"Jace, just go look for yourself. He's in the bedroom."

The sheriff spotted the vomit on the steps and sneered.

"Make sure he stays put," he muttered, and Kara grinned, flipping the thumb snap on her pistol.

Lane had no intention of moving. He still wasn't sure he could if he wanted. He sat and listened as the sheriff's heavy boots thumped across the floors. He heard the creak of a door and then –

"Son of a bitch!"

"I told you," Lane whimpered, looking down at his hands. "I fucking told you."

THREE

Connor holds my hand while he drives. It's been two months since Mark, and we're both in the mood. My brother gets fidgety after a while, so it helps if we can touch one another.

Skin-to-skin is essential. People need that.

But not in the same way we do. Our first memory is of the moments between our births. We were ripped from each other.

I had to wait three whole minutes for Caleb to get here.

And we've been together ever since. I know what you're thinking. Oooo, it's that creepy psychic thing all twins have.

Bullshit.

Exactly. Not all twins are connected the way we are. We're special.

Very special.

Unique.

* * *

WE'VE BEEN DRIVING A LOT, BUNKING DOWN AT CHEAP MOTELS THAT DON'T ASK QUESTIONS. AND WE DON'T REALLY GIVE THEM A REASON TO. WE GET OUR ROOM AND STAY QUIET.

WE ALMOST TOOK THE GUY WORKING THE COUNTER AT THE LAST PLACE. HE HAD EYES FOR US AS SOON AS WE WALKED INTO THE OFFICE. HE WAS HANDSOME WITH BLUE EYES AND A LITTLE SCRUFF ALONG HIS JAW. WE USUALLY DON'T BREAK OUR ROUTINE, STICK TO THE BARS, IN AND OUT, BUT I WANTED HIM AS SOON AS I SAW HIM.

"Need a room?" he asked, clearing his throat.

CONNOR AND I LOOKED AT EACH OTHER AND SMILED.

"YEAH, WE'VE BEEN DRIVING A LONG TIME TODAY. JUST NEED A HOT SHOWER AND A BED."

"Two beds?"

NOW, WHAT MADE HIM ASK THAT?

"I MEAN, WE'RE FINE WITH ONE SO LONG AS IT'S A BIG BED," I SAID.

"SOMETHING WITH ROOM ENOUGH FOR TWO…"

"… OR THREE."

He visibly shuddered and cleared his throat again, pulling out an old-fashioned ledger.

"I, uh, yeah … you could take the room on the corner at the end of the row here. It's got a nice, big bed."

I LOOKED OVER AT CALEB, WHO GAVE ME AN ALMOST IMPERCEPTIBLE SMILE.

I COULD ALREADY TASTE HIM. HE WASN'T EMOTIONALLY WRECKED LIKE MARK. YOU ALMOST HEAR HIS HEARTBEAT; IT WAS SO FAST IN HIS CHEST. MARK WAS LOOKING TO FORGET. THE CLERK WANTED TO KNOW, AND THAT'S AN ENTIRELY DIFFERENT THING. LITTLE BEADS OF SWEAT BROKE OUT ON HIS FOREHEAD AS HE FUMBLED FOR A PEN. IT WAS PRECIOUS IN A WAY. THERE WAS AN AIR OF INNOCENT AROUSAL IN THE AIR AND OUR MOUTHS WATERED AT IT.

"WHAT'S YOUR NAME?"

"What?"

"YOUR NAME," I REPEATED AND LEANED A LITTLE CLOSER TO HIM. "YOU HAVE ONE, RIGHT?"

"Um, yeah, yeah, it's Ryan."

"NICE TO MEET YOU, RYAN. I'M CALEB, AND HE'S CONNOR."

"Cool," he says.

I signed his book, never taking my eyes off him and Caleb. He was taking the bait all right.

"So," I said. "The key?"

"Huh?"

"The key ... to the room."

"Oh! Yeah, sorry."

He turned his back to us, and I stepped closer to Caleb, putting my arm around his waist as he did the same. Ryan did a double-take when he turned back to hand over the key.

"Kind of a slow night for you, isn't it?"

"Um."

"There's only one car in the lot besides ours."

"Yeah, we're ... not many ...."

"You should walk us down to our room."

"I ... what?"

Connor leaned his head close to mine.

"Walk us to our room," he said.

"I've got to watch … in case …."

"No, you don't," I corrected. "No one else is going to come in tonight. You know it."

Ryan was in a daze when he stepped out of the office in front of us. Caleb and I held onto each other, still walking behind him. We smiled when he looked back at us as he turned to unlock the room.

"Go on," I said. "We're right here."

He stepped into the room and walked to the side of the bed to switch on one of the three small lamps in the room. Caleb pulled the door closed behind us. We stood, looking at each other for a moment.

"Well?"

"What?"

I looked at Caleb, raising an eyebrow.

I smiled at Connor and stepped toward Ryan. He was shorter than us, maybe five foot seven, and I could smell cologne up close. Nothing overpowering, subtle, like him.

"RYAN," I SAID, "IT MUST GET LONELY OUT HERE AT NIGHT. ALL ALONE. NO ONE TO TALK TO. NOTHING TO DO BUT WATCH BAD LATE-NIGHT TV IN THE OFFICE."

"I read," he said, swallowing hard.

"READING IS GOOD. SMART PEOPLE READ. SMART PEOPLE ARE A REAL TURN-ON."

"Uh, they are?"

"OH YES," I WHISPERED. "RYAN, HAVE YOU EVER BEEN WITH A MAN BEFORE?"

"I-I, yes."

"HAVE YOU EVER BEEN WITH TWO?"

"No ...."

HIS VOICE WAS SO SMALL, SO FULL OF NEED.

"BUT YOU'VE ALWAYS WANTED TO TRY IT, RIGHT?" I TRACED MY FINGERS ALONG HIS JAW, FEELING LIGHT STUBBLE AS IT PRICKED AT MY FINGERS. HE DIDN'T SAY ANYTHING. MAYBE HE COULDN'T. HE JUST NODDED. I SLID MY HAND UNDER HIS SHIRT AND OVER HIS SMOOTH, FLAT BELLY, AND HE TREMBLED BENEATH MY FINGERS. I LEANED IN, KISSED HIS NECK GENTLY, AND NIBBLED UP TO HIS EAR.

HE MANAGED A MOAN IN RESPONSE.

"I THOUGHT SO," I PURRED INTO HIS EAR. "AND LOOK AT YOU ... TWO FOR THE PRICE OF ONE. YOU'VE GOT TO BE THE LUCKIEST MOTEL CLERK THIS SIDE OF EL PASO."

CALEB HELD HIS HAND OUT TO ME, AND I MOVED TO THE OTHER SIDE OF RYAN. I STARED INTO THE EYES OF MY TWIN FOR TWO SECONDS BEFORE WE BOTH LEANED IN TO KISS HIS NECK THIS TIME. HE YELPED WHEN I NIPPED HIS JAW, BUT HE DIDN'T PULL AWAY.

I SLIPPED A HAND DOWN HIS PANTS, GRABBING ONTO HIS STIFFENING COCK. THE HEAD WAS ALREADY SLICK, AND HE TREMBLED WHEN I RAN MY THUMB OVER IT.

RYAN TURNED HIS FACE TO MINE, AND I KISSED HIM. HE TASTED LIKE CINNAMON CANDY AND MENTHOL CIGARETTES, A SURPRISINGLY DELICIOUS COMBINATION. SO MUCH SO THAT I MOANED WHEN CONNOR TURNED THE CLERK'S FACE TOWARD HIM. I NEEDED SOMETHING FROM THIS MAN IN MY MOUTH. WITH MY FREE HAND, I PUSHED UP HIS SHIRT AND GRABBED THE NIPPLE CLOSEST TO ME. EVERY MUSCLE IN HIS TORSO FLINCHED AND TENSED, AND HE GROANED INTO MY TWIN'S MOUTH. I COULD SEE THE SMALLEST TUFT OF HAIR FROM HIS ARMPIT AT THIS ANGLE. I WANTED TO PRESS MY NOSE INTO IT. SMELL THE NATURAL SCENT OF HIM. I WAS JUST ABOUT TO WHEN A LOUD HORN BLEW OUTSIDE THE MOTEL.

RYAN JERKED, PULLING HIS MOUTH AWAY FROM MINE. HIS LIPS WERE RED AND SWOLLEN FROM OUR KISSES.

"I ... HOLD ON," HE SAID.

HE MANAGED TO FREE HIMSELF FROM OUR GRASP AND RAN TO
THE WINDOW TO LOOK OUT INTO THE NIGHT.

"Shit," he groaned. "I've got customers. I have to go."

"NO, YOU DON'T," CALEB PROTESTED, AND WE WATCHED A
SILENT WAR GOING ON BEHIND THE CLERK'S EYES. HIS DESIRE
BURNED HOT THERE, AND FOR A MOMENT, I THOUGHT HE'D
ACQUIESCE AS HE LOOKED FROM CALEB'S FACE TO MINE. THEN,
THE LIGHT WENT OUT. HE TURNED AND BOLTED FROM THE ROOM,
NOT EVEN BOTHERING TO CLOSE THE DOOR BEHIND HIM.
CALEB STARTED TO FOLLOW HIM, BUT I HELD HIM BACK.

"HE'S GONE. YOU KNOW WE CAN'T GO AFTER THEM IF THEY RUN
LIKE THAT. REMEMBER SAN ANTONIO?"

I FROZE IN CONNOR'S ARMS. I DID REMEMBER SAN ANTONIO.
THIS AMAZINGLY HOT TOURIST HAD A FIGHT WITH HIS WIFE.
WE PICKED HIM UP IN A TOURIST TRAP CANTINA. WE WENT TO
A CHEAP LITTLE MOTEL, NOT SO DIFFERENT FROM THIS ONE.
THINGS WERE JUST GETTING GOOD WHEN HIS PHONE STARTED
RINGING.

WE TRIED TO GET HIM TO IGNORE IT, BUT AFTER THE THIRD CALL,
HE PULLED HIMSELF AWAY FROM US. WE LISTENED TO HIM LIE
TO HIS WIFE ABOUT WHERE HE WAS. WATCHED AS HE STARTED
PULLING UP HIS PANTS. I TRIED TO STOP HIM, BUT HE SWATTED
MY HAND AWAY. THEN HE HUNG UP AND TOLD US HE HAD TO

LEAVE. I FOLLOWED HIM OUT INTO THE LOT. I THOUGHT I COULD CONVINCE HIM TO COME BACK.

THE BASTARD PUNCHED ME. HARD ENOUGH TO BREAK A RIB. BEFORE I COULD EVEN REGISTER WHAT HAPPENED, CALEB WAS OUT OF THE MOTEL ROOM AND ONTO THE GUY. THEY WERE FIGHTING IN THE PARKING LOT, WHICH DREW A CROWD FAST. CALEB DREW HIS RAZOR AND WAS ABOUT TO USE IT WHEN THE NIGHT CLERK APPEARED OUT OF NOWHERE WITH A GUN.

HE ORDERED US ALL OFF THE PROPERTY, AND IT WAS ONLY THEN THAT WE REALIZED HOW MUCH ATTENTION WE'D DRAWN TO OURSELVES.

IN OUR ENTIRE LIVES, WE CAN COUNT THE NUMBER OF MISTAKES WE'VE MADE ON ONE HAND. SAN ANTONIO WAS ONE OF THEM. NOT ONLY DID WE MAKE A SPECTACLE OF OURSELVES, BUT WE LOST OUR LOVER, AND BECAUSE OF MY INJURIES, WE MADE A NEW RULE.

IF A GUY LEAVES US OF HIS OWN FREE WILL, THEN WE TAKE IT AS A SIGN HE'S NOT SUPPOSED TO BE OURS.

WE DON'T REALLY BELIEVE IN GOD MUCH, BUT WE DO BELIEVE THERE'S SOMETHING OUT THERE. HOW ELSE WOULD WE HAVE BEEN MADE WHAT WE ARE?

I FROWNED AT CALEB AND NODDED MY HEAD. I HOPED RYAN WOULD RETURN, BUT I KNEW HE WOULDN'T. THE NERVOUS LITTLE RABBIT HAD ESCAPED THE FOXES.

* * *

"DO YOU THINK WE'LL BE ABLE TO FIND SOMEONE SOON?" I
WONDER OUT LOUD.

"OF COURSE, WE WILL," I REASSURE CALEB, SQUEEZING HIS
HAND. "WE'LL STOP IN THE NEXT TOWN. HOW ABOUT THAT?"

"I'D LIKE THAT," HE WHISPERS TO ME AND SLIDES ACROSS THE
SEAT TO SIT NEXT TO ME, LAYING HIS HEAD ON MY SHOULDER.

"SO WOULD I," I ANSWER. "WHY DON'T YOU TAKE A NAP? IT'LL
BE GOOD FOR US."

HE SQUEEZES MY HAND THIS TIME, AND IN MOMENTS, HIS
BREATHING BEGINS TO EVEN OUT. OF COURSE, I DON'T NEED HIS
BREATHING TO TELL CALEB WAS ASLEEP. I COULD FEEL IT. A PART
OF ME FALLS SILENT AND RELAXED. SO LONG AS HE CONTINUES TO
SLEEP, WE'LL BOTH BE FULLY REFRESHED WHEN WE STOP FOR THE
NIGHT.

READY TO SEDUCE.

I TURN MY FACE TO THE SIDE, KISS HIS FOREHEAD, AND BEGIN TO
HUM A LULLABY AS THE TEXAS SUN SLOWLY SLIPS TOWARD THE
HORIZON.

FOUR

LANE CURSED AT the ding from the truck's dashboard, signaling low fuel. He should have stopped in the last town, but he couldn't. He needed to keep moving. He was getting close. He could feel it. Fortunately for him, in this part of Texas, the towns were all about fifteen to twenty miles apart. He willed the truck to keep going as he crossed the city limits into Clarendon.

He frowned at the large cross next to the welcome sign and again as he saw another and another along the main strip through town.

"What the hell?"

Everywhere he looked were church signs and Bible verses. They hung from storefronts and beckoned from street corners. He spotted a gas station and pulled in next to the pumps. He was out of the truck and removing the gas cap in a flash. He did not want to spend any more time in this town than he had to. It was creepy.

The sign on the pump flashed after he swiped his card, and he pulled the trigger on the hose, flicking the tab down to lock it in place before making his way into the store. Cool air-conditioning greeted him, and of course, church music played from unseen speakers.

"Welcome, weary traveler," the man behind the counter said in greeting.

He was all of five foot five and probably clocked in at just under three hundred pounds with greying hair and a smile so wide it contorted his face. His sweat-stained polo shirt had seen better days, but a brightly colored button on his shirt announced, "This is the day the Lord has made."

"Are you for real?"

The question was out of his mouth before he could stop it, and he immediately held up a hand in apology.

"I'm sorry. Just been a long day."

"That's quite all right, son. I know what it is to be tired."

"Restroom?"

"In the back."

The smile never faltered on the older man's face. Lane could swear it followed him around the corner and down a hall where two doors stood. One read "Shepherds," and the other was "Lambs." He shook his head at the signs but decided he was a shepherd anyway. He pushed the door open and locked it behind him.

He smiled when he saw the graffiti on the walls. At least something about this place was normal. Just above the urinal, someone named Robbie listed all the things he'd do for twenty dollars. Someone had tried to scribble over it, but they weren't very effective. If Robbie could do half the things he said, the man was going places. Beneath the advertisement, someone scrawled "The rainbow belongs to god, not perverts" in red ink.

Lane winced and shut his eyes, listening to the sound of his own pee hitting the porcelain surface of the urinal.

Pervert.

That's what the Sheriff had called Mark when they got the DNA results back from the blood and ... other stuff ... on the scene. Mark had had a good time right up until the moment he died. They found three different sets of DNA on the scene. The weird thing was that two of the sets were almost identical. The medical examiner had explained to them that meant the other two men were most likely twins.

That was all Jace Winters needed to hear. He closed the case in three days, and when Lane had confronted him about it, the Sheriff laid it all out for him.

"The way I see it, your buddy was a god-damned pervert. He probably lured those boys out to his place and got rough with them. Maybe he was afraid they'd talk. Maybe he just didn't want anyone knowing what he got up to, including the people he got up to it with. He got rough with them, and they defended themselves."

"That makes no god-damned sense, Jace."

"It does if I say it does."

The two men stared each other down for a long time until Jace finally pushed his cowboy hat back on his head and grinned.

"You two were friends for a long time, weren't you?"

"You know we were. What the hell's that got to do with anything?"

"I'm just surprised you didn't know what he got up to. Maybe you did know. Maybe you liked some of the same things?"

Lane felt the weight of the Sheriff's words land on his shoulders, and he took a step back.

"Seems to me," Jace continued, "that if you don't want certain things getting around, you might just leave well enough alone. Go home. Mourn your friend. And keep your fucking mouth shut."

He was ashamed of himself that day. His friend had been killed, and he tucked tail and ran home at the implication someone

— anyone — would think *he* was a pervert, too. He sat in his double-wide drinking for two days. The more he drank, the angrier he got until it finally boiled over. He broke every piece of glass in his house, put his fist through walls, and cursed so loud one of his neighbors came beating on his door. He convinced the man to go back home. He took a shower, packed a bag, and left home behind that night, determined to find the men who killed Mark.

By the following morning, he was just south of Dallas. He pulled into a diner for something to eat and called up Tommy, who ran Mark's favorite bar. He had to call three times before the man picked up the phone.

"What?!"

"Tommy," he said. "it's Lane."

"Lane who?"

"Wake up, Tommy."

"Fuck you."

"Come on, man. I need to as you a couple of questions about Mark Haskell."

"I don't know nothing," the man grunted.

"Bullshit. Look, you don't have to point any fingers. I just need you to answer one question."

There was a long pause on the other side of the connection. Lane would have thought the call had been dropped if he couldn't hear Tommy's labored breathing.

"You got one," he said finally.

"All I want to know is if you saw a set of twins talking to Mark at the bar that night."

"What?"

"Twins, Tommy. A set of twins. Guys."

"Oh, those two," Tommy muttered.

"Tommy Dwayne, you listen. I need to know whatever you can tell me."

"There were two of them," he said stupidly.

"No shit."

"They were taller, about six feet. Black hair. Green eyes. They had a few beers with Mark, except I never actually saw either one of them drink."

"Tommy, did they leave the bar together?"

"No."

"Fuck," Lane whispered.

"I mean, they left at the same time, but not really together, you know?"

Lane sat up in the booth and leaned over the sticky table.

"Okay, did you get their names?"

"That's two questions," Tommy said.

"Fuck you, Tommy. Did you get their names?"

"I heard them talking, but I don't remember, okay?"

Lane ran his hand through his hair, then held up a finger to the waitress to indicate he needed another minute.

He counted to ten.

"Thanks, Tommy."

"I'm sorry, man. Did they —"

"I don't know," Lane answered, "but I'm going to find out."

He'd been on the road ever since, driving from town to town. He knew the likelihood of finding his friend's killers was small, but he had to try. Someone had to try.

He'd gotten close a couple of times. So, he thought anyway, but he was getting close now. He could feel it. Things were falling into place.

He finished up and washed his hands before stepping back

into the store proper. He grabbed sodas and snacks and took them to the counter, where the smiling man scanned and bagged things up for him.

"You don't mind me saying so," the man said, "you look lost."

Lane sighed.

"Not lost. Just … I'm working on it."

The man nodded and held out his hand.

"Ralph," he said.

He shook the offered hand.

"Lane."

"Glad to meet you, Lane. Listen, I'm not gonna preach at ya. I'm just gonna slip a couple of these tracts in your bag. You do with 'em what you want. Also, here's a card for my brother's motel. If you need a place to rest, the door is always open. My nephew Ryan helps him run the place. You just tell 'em I sent you, and they'll give you a discount."

Lane smiled and dropped the card into his pocket.

"Thanks."

"You're welcome! You have a blessed day, now!"

"I … thanks again," he said, picking up his bags and stepping back out into the heat. He checked his watch. It was getting late. He pulled the card out of his pocket as he settled in behind the wheel, then punched the address into his phone. It was only ten miles out the way, and he could use a shower and a real bed.

He tapped "Begin Route" on the screen and pulled out onto the street.

* * *

DUST SWIRLED IN the evening breeze as Lane pulled into the parking lot of the Sleepaway Lodge. There were only two other cars in the lot, and he assumed the one parked next to the office belonged to the owner. He sat in the darkened cab for a minute, rubbing his eyes and yawning. He hadn't been sleeping enough. It wasn't from a lack of trying, but the middle of the night was worst for him. His stupid brain wouldn't shut up.

A chime drew his attention to his phone. He tapped the screen to clear the map he'd followed to the motel and looked at the text from Jessica.

Where are you?

He sighed, considered answering, then tapped again to hide the notification.

Like most everyone he knew, Jessica didn't understand why he was out wandering aimlessly looking for the men Mark spent his last night with. She'd bought Jace's story because she wanted to believe it. He knew, deep down, that it made her feel better about herself somehow for leaving Mark. Her absolution was granted one platitude at a time from well-meaning friends who told her she was right to have left him. Most got around to implying that Mark might have intentionally hurt her eventually. Others outright told her she was lucky to have escaped without "catching something you can't wash off."

It turned his stomach, and the more she rolled in that muck, the more he hated her.

Lane stuffed the phone into his pocket as he exited the truck. The creaked when he shut it behind him, and a swell of cicadas called from the dark beyond the motel lot. He took the three steps to the office door and pulled it open, shielding his eyes from the artificial lights.

A young man stood behind the counter with a strained smile on his face. He was shorter than Lane, but not by much, with blonde hair that fell flat around his face down to his collar. He had the pronounced Adam's apple of a gangly sixteen-year-old, and Lane was sure he only had to shave once a week … maybe. Still, there was something about him.

"Hi," the young man said. "I'm Ryan. Welcome to the Sleepaway Lodge. Need a room?"

"Thanks," Lane answered. "I definitely do. I met your uncle Ralph at a convenience store. He recommended the place."

He didn't imagine Ryan's smile tightening.

"Well, we'll have to thank him the next time we see him. You have the pick of the place except for twenty-two."

"Doesn't matter to me so long as it's quiet and has a hot shower."

"You get all the quiet you want out here except for the cicadas. Not much I can do about them."

Lane grinned. He liked the guy. He had a certain charm to him. He stepped up to the counter and pulled out his wallet, handing over a credit card he was almost certain had enough space for the room for a one-nighter in a place like this. Ryan's fingertips grazed his own as he took the card, and a little electric charge shot between them.

Lane hissed and jerked his hand back.

"Storm's coming," Ryan said quietly, turning to run the card. Lane watched and smiled to himself when the green light flashed and a receipt slowly printed from the machine.

"Didn't see any clouds out there."

"Don't have to. You just have to feel it," Ryan replied, turning back to him with a pen and the room receipt.

Lane nodded that he understood with a knowing grin and bent to sign the receipt.

The counter was scattered with papers and pamphlets on local history. Just beneath the room ledger, his eyes slid over what looked like a drawing. Black hair and green eyes. He paused, looking at it. When Ryan turned back to the wall to grab a room key, he used a single finger to pull it farther from under the book. He revealed enough to see the shoulder of someone else when Ryan's hand fell over the drawing, pushing it back under the ledger.

"That's private," he whispered, and Lane held his hands up, stepping back.

"Sorry."

Ryan's smile came back, forced and strained.

"No problem. You're in room one. Next door. No need in having to move your truck. It's also got the best water pressure. Closest to the tank."

"Thanks," he replied, sighing. "You have a good night."

"You, too. You let me know if you need anything.

FIVE

RYAN WAITED UNTIL he heard the door of the stranger's room open and close before he slid the drawing from under the ledger on the counter. He stared down into the dark green eyes of the twins and frowned. He still hadn't quite gotten them right.

There were nights since their meeting when he could think of nothing but the smell of their skin. The warmth of their touch. The feel of their mouths on his neck, jaw, ears, and lips. He relived each moment in the privacy of his apartment, fantasizing about where it could have gone, what they would have been like together.

There were mornings he couldn't fall asleep until he'd fulfilled his fantasies two and three times, fantasizing about different positions and sexual permutations, wearing himself out, cumming again and again until they finally faded enough to allow him to sleep. Some days, he wanted to be between them. Others, he wanted to be fucked while one of the brothers fucked the other.

His face flushed, and he turned away from the drawing, fidgeting with the TV remote.

Ryan heard the shower next door turn on, and he thought of the man in the room. He was taller than him, with sun-streaked brown hair and tanned skin. The stubble on his chin and cheek looked rough, and he wondered what it would feel like next to his own smooth skin, wondered what his body looked like beneath the worn t-shirt and jeans.

He frowned, shook his head, and focused on the television. The classic movies station saved his sanity on long, slow nights at the motel. It was easy to slip into black-and-white worlds, and it wasn't long before he was entirely engrossed in a movie that was already halfway over when he found it. He sat watching Bette Davis face off with a man he assumed was her husband. He had the feeling Bette's character had killed someone. It seemed like something she'd do.

Time slipped by, and he checked the lot less and less. The movie had reached its dramatic climax. Bette had killed the man, all right, but not for the reason everyone thought. He was leaning close to the screen when it suddenly went black, and he saw the stranger's reflection in its glass.

He stood up, falling back from the man. What was his name? Lane, that was it. Lane looked pissed, and he was holding up the drawing of the twins.

"Who are they?" he asked. His voice was barely a whisper.

"I ... what?"

"I said, who are they?"

Ryan's eyes flickered between the drawing and Lane. The man's wet hair was dripping onto the counter. He wore a tank top now, and his shoulders and biceps were defined. The clerk had no doubt this guy could whip his ass in a heartbeat.

"It's ... just a drawing," Ryan murmured.

"Bullshit."

"It is!"

Lane stepped around the counter, holding the drawing out in front of him like a weapon or shield or some kind of combination of the two. His eyes were steel, and Ryan could feel the anger radiating from his skin. He was terrified this man was about to hurt him or worse. He couldn't fathom why he'd be interested in the drawing, couldn't imagine why it had enraged him.

"Please," he said after a moment. "Please, don't hurt me. I'll tell you whatever you want."

Slowly, little by little, he watched the tension fade. His grey eyes softened from steel to storm clouds. His jaw loosened. He began to lower his hands and stand from his crouching, ready-to-fight stance.

It was now or never.

With more grace than he ever expected from himself, Ryan grabbed the small container of mace from beneath the counter and sprayed it into Lane's face. The man immediately shouted, closing his eyes, and falling back and away. Ryan ducked, trying to avoid Lane's swinging arms. It should have been an easy escape, except that when he'd clenched his fists, Lane had crumpled the drawing of the twins.

Ryan faltered, upset by the damage. Lane's fist connected with his face in that split second, and the world went black.

* * *

"HEY. HEY, WAKE up."

The voice sounded like it was coming from far away. It certainly couldn't be in the dark with him. This place was quiet. Peaceful. The voice was harsh, and Ryan turned away from it. He wanted to dive deeper into the voice but found he could not. Something had grabbed him and pulled him back toward the surface. He flailed his arms and legs when his head broke through the surface, and the world filled with too-bright lights and the demands of a voice he only barely knew.

"Ryan, right? Ryan, are you okay? Wake up, man."

Ryan's eyelids fluttered open. He blinked them repeatedly, looking for something, anything he recognized in the sudden return of sound and light. Someone grabbed his wrists, and as he focused, he realized it was Lane. The man's face sharpened in front of him. His eyes were swollen, red, and it took a moment for Ryan to remember the mace he'd unloaded on the stranger.

"Get off me," he slurred, pushing the bigger man away. "Get the fuck off me."

Lane shook his head, but he let go of him and took a step back to give him room to right himself. Ryan sat up and looked down at his rumpled clothes. A single drop of red stuck out like a beacon on his white t-shirt. He wiped at it but only managed to smear the blood.

"Whose is it?" he asked, hopefully.

"Yours, kid."

"Not a kid."

Lane looked at him and bit the inside of his lip.

"No," he admitted, "you're not. Want a hand up?"

Ryan considered and, after a moment, stuck out his left to take Lane's offered right. The office spun briefly when he was on his feet, but the vertigo passed quickly. He righted the stool he'd knocked over in the corner and took a seat, staring at the man who now stood on the other side of the counter from him.

"I'm ... sorry," Lane said with a shrug. "I came in way too hot and heavy. That's on me."

He laid the drawing between them. The paper was torn down the middle separating the twins, and Ryan frowned at the sight of it. He did his best to smooth out the paper and sighed.

"Sorry about that, too," Lane offered. "That must have taken some time to do."

"A bit," Ryan admitted. "But I needed to start over anyway."

"I ... look, there's no easy way to ask this, but do you know these guys, or are they something you dreamed up?"

Ryan considered. It was a great question. "Some days, I'm not sure," he admitted. "They ... came to the motel a while ago. They just stayed the one night."

Lane eased forward, leaning over the drawing. "Did they ... you ... did anything happen?"

Tears glistened in the sea of blue in Ryan's eyes when he looked up. "Almost."

He told the stranger everything. It was easy once he got started. He didn't know Lane, so it didn't matter what the man thought of him. What's more, the man seemed to empathize when he explained how the twins had seduced him, about how much he'd wanted to be with them. His face burned when he said it out loud, but not from shame.

His story told, Ryan lapsed into silence, and Lane stepped back from the counter, giving him room to breathe.

"You got an ice machine?"

"Huh?"

"Your cheek is swelling. The ice will help."

"Oh," Ryan said. "Yeah, in the alcove down the walk here. I'll go get some."

"No, you sit. Relax. I'll be right back."

Ryan didn't protest. He laid his head on the counter and floated until Lane returned with a bucket of ice and one of the hand towels from his room. He watched him lay the towel out, folding it just so, creating a pocket for the ice before twisting the cloth and handing over the makeshift ice pack. It felt good against the heat in Ryan's cheek.

He narrowed his eyes and looked into the man's eyes. "You've done this before?"

"More times than you can count."

"So, why are you looking for them?"

"I don't know that I am. I just know that they fit the description of the men I *am* looking for, and with what you've told me, I might be right."

"You didn't answer the question."

Lane looked at him, frowned, then sighed. "*If* they are who I think they are, they killed my best friend."

Ryan's eyes widened. He'd spent hours considering why the twins would have chosen him. Murder never crossed his mind. "I don't think they'd do that."

"Why? Because they got you all hot and bothered?"

"No, they … why would they?"

"I don't know. That's what I want to find out."

"And if they did?"

"The sheriff back home doesn't care much. Didn't spend more than a couple weeks looking. If the law isn't interested, I figure no one will care if I kill them."

"If they didn't?"

"Then I keep looking."

Silence settled between them. Ryan was conflicted, unsure what to think of Lane's plans. The one thing he did know was that the twins wouldn't be easy to kill. There was something about them. He couldn't name it. Couldn't point to a particular characteristic. Hell, he didn't really know them at all, but deep down in his guts, he knew they could take care of themselves.

What Lane said could very well be true. Anything was possible, but he couldn't let them be killed, not before he could see them again, touch them. Reaffirm to himself they were real.

Could he warn them about Lane's plans? Maybe.

Would he? He didn't know.

He looked across the counter at the other man and considered him. Lane had strong shoulders and arms. His chest was broad and covered in fine dark hair that peeked from beneath his tank top. His stubbled jaw was square and set. The lines around his eyes were the only hint that he was older, though Ryan guessed he might be forty at most. It was his eyes, though, that captured and held Ryan's attention.

Stormy grey and far deeper than he would have expected from most men who looked and carried themselves like Lane. He was a man on a mission, and Ryan would have laid money on the counter that the man couldn't explain exactly why. Perhaps he just needed answers, a reason. Perhaps, he really meant to kill someone.

He sighed.

"I'm coming with you," he whispered, then cleared his throat and repeated the statement.

"Like hell," Lane protested, but Ryan held up a hand.

"Of the two of us, I'm the only one that's seen them. Even with my drawings, you'll have a time being certain, and that's if you find them at all. Sounds like you've been driving aimlessly for a while now and barely got lucky tonight. I'm coming with you. I can help."

Lane cocked his head to the side.

"Why?"

"I … if they meant to kill me, then I have my own debts to settle."

The other man considered him a moment, then nodded.

"Won't you be missed here?"

"Yeah, dad will be pissed, but I don't think he'll fire me. Family business and all."

Lane stood to his full height, and for a moment, Ryan thought he'd refuse. Then, he held out a hand to him across the counter, and they shook. His grip was firm, and the callouses sent shivers down Ryan's spine.

"First light?" the man asked.

"Dad shows up at seven. We'll need to be gone before then. Go sleep for a bit. I'll be ready."

Lane nodded at him and left him alone in the office.

A few hours later, they were on the highway. He left a note for his dad on the counter and turned off his phone. He didn't want to deal with him right away. Storm clouds were gathering over the road.

Ryan fell asleep as the first drops of rain splashed against the windshield.

SIX

SMALL TOWNS ARE UNDENIABLY THE BEST HUNTING GROUNDS.

NOT BECAUSE THE MEN ARE SEXIER, OR THE LOCATIONS ARE MORE
SECLUDED.

IT'S BECAUSE MOST PEOPLE IN LITTLE TEXAS TOWNS ARE ALL
TOO HAPPY TO LOOK THE OTHER WAY WHEN MURDERS ARE
COMPLICATED BY QUEERNESS. THE CLOSEST WE HAVE EVER COME
TO BEING CAUGHT WAS IN A LARGE CITY WHERE MINDS ARE MORE
OPEN AND RELIGION HOLDS LESS SWAY.

AS SOON AS A LOCAL SHERIFF'S DEPARTMENT REALIZES THAT A
"CRIME" INVOLVES A SEXUAL COMPONENT.

LIKE TWO OR MORE MEN FUCKING EACH OTHER.

THEY QUIETLY CLOSE THEIR FILES AND LOCK THEM AWAY.

BUT NOT BEFORE WORD GETS OUT.

THE COMMUNITY TAKES CARE OF THE REST.
THEY CLOSE RANKS, SHOCKED THAT SOMETHING LIKE THIS COULD
EVEN HAPPEN IN THEIR TOWN. THEY CLUTCH THEIR PEARLS

AND PRACTICE THEIR SAD, SYMPATHETIC LOOKS IN CASE THEY MEET THE DEAD MAN'S FAMILY AT THE LOCAL GROCERY STORE. THEY PUT ON THEIR BLACK MOURNING CLOTHES AND CROWD THE FUNERAL HOME, NOT TO MOURN BUT TO GAWK AND GOSSIP AND SHAKE THEIR HEADS AT A CORPSE WHO CANNOT SEE THEM.

THEN, WITHIN A WEEK OR TWO OF THE BURIAL, THE TONGUES REALLY BEGIN TO WAG. OLD FRIENDS SUDDENLY REMEMBER THINGS THEY NOW LABEL CLUES TO THE TRUE IDENTITY OF THE MEN THEY'VE KNOWN FOR YEARS. FORMER GIRLFRIENDS SHARE STORIES THEY MAKE UP ON THE SPOT ABOUT STRANGE REQUESTS THE MEN HAD IN THE BEDROOM WHILE SHOCKED FRIENDS SHAKE THEIR HEADS IN SAD COMMISERATION.

LOCAL PASTORS SUDDENLY HAVE BRAND NEW FODDER FOR THEIR SERMONS. THEY PREACH THEIR FERVENT HOMOPHOBIA FROM THE PULPIT AND REMIND THE CONGREGATION OF LEVITICUS.

"IF A MAN LIES WITH A MAN AS HE SHOULD LIE WITH A WOMAN, HE SHALL BE TAKEN OUT OF THE CITY AND STONED. HIS BLOOD IS ON HIS OWN HANDS."

AND THE CONGREGATION SHOUTS VEHEMENT "A-MENS" AND "HALLELUJAHS" COLORED BY GOD-AFFIRMED HATE.

WITHIN A MONTH, WE HAVE FADED INTO THE BACKGROUND, FORGOTTEN BY THE POPULATION. THEY ONLY HAVE EYES AND JUDGMENT FOR THE MEN IN THEIR COMMUNITY WHO THEY DECIDE LIED TO THEM, NEVER REALIZING THAT THEY ARE THE REASON THE LIES WERE TOLD. EVEN IF WE WEREN'T SO VERY GOOD AT

WHAT WE DO, WE COULD CONTINUE DOING IT, NOT DESPITE BUT BECAUSE OF THEM.

* * *

"WHERE ARE WE?" I ASK, LIFTING MY HEAD FROM CONNOR'S SHOULDER AS HE SHUTS OFF THE ENGINE.

"BORGER," HE RESPONDS. "THE BUDGET INN."

"HUNGRY," I MUMBLE. I CAN FEEL HIS GRIN WITHOUT LOOKING AT HIM.

"ME, TOO, BUT FIRST WE SHOWER."

"YES," I AGREE, STRETCHING.

CONNOR MAKES SHORT WORK OF RENTING A ROOM. THE MIDDLE-AGED WOMAN BEHIND THE COUNTER STARES JUST A LITTLE TOO LONG AT US, BUT SHE DOESN'T SAY MUCH. KEY IN HAND, WE HEAD TO THE ROOM.

IT'S NOT MUCH, BUT IT'LL DO FOR A NIGHT OR TWO. THE DOUBLE BEDS ARE COVERED IN COMFORTERS THAT WERE MOST DEFINITELY CHOSEN SOMETIME AROUND 1980 BECAUSE THEY WERE CHEAP AND DURABLE.

WE DON'T SPEAK. WE DROP OUR BAGS, STRIP DOWN, AND HEAD FOR THE BATHROOM WITH OUR TOILETRIES BAG IN TOW.

THERE IS NOTHING COLDER THAN BATHROOM TILE IN A MOTEL. I DON'T KNOW HOW THEY DO IT. THE REST OF THE ROOM MIGHT BE HOT AND HUMID, BUT THOSE BATHROOM TILES ARE ALWAYS CHILLY. CONNOR TURNS THE WATER ON HOT ENOUGH TO REDDEN OUR SKIN, THEN SMILES, HOLDING OUT A HAND TO ME, AND WE STEP UNDER THE SPRAY TOGETHER.

I POUR SHAMPOO INTO EACH OF OUR HANDS AND BEGIN TO MASSAGE IT INTO CALEB'S SCALP AS HE DOES MINE. BOTH THE SHAMPOO AND OUR CONDITIONER HAVE MENTHOL ADDED TO THEM. IT TINGLES WHEN IT MAKES CONTACT WITH THE SCALP. IT WORKS WONDERS IN THE TEXAS SUMMER TO COMBAT THE HEAT, BUT IT ALSO LEAVES OUR HAIR SHINY AND SMELLS UNMISTAKABLY MASCULINE. THE LATHER IS FRAGRANT, AND FURTHER RELAXES US AS WE DIRECT THE SPRAY INTO EACH OTHER'S HAIR TO RINSE IT AWAY. I LOVE THE WAY CALEB SIGHS.

OUR BODY WASH IS SCENTED WITH SANDALWOOD AND THE BAREST HINT OF PATCHOULI, AGAIN A DECIDEDLY MASCULINE SPICY SCENT THAT WE BOTH ENJOY, AND WE TAKE OUR TIME LATHERING EACH OTHER'S BODIES, MASSAGING ROAD-STIFF MUSCLES.

THE STEAM SMELLS LIKE MINT AND SANDALWOOD WHEN I GET DOWN ON MY KNEES IN FRONT OF CONNOR. HE PUTS HIS HANDS BEHIND HIS HEAD WITH HIS BACK TO THE SHOWERHEAD AND SPREADS HIS LEGS JUST A LITTLE.

I GENTLY MOVE HIS COCK BACK AND FORTH, CHECKING FOR ANY SIGN OF INFECTION. WARTS, SORES, ANYTHING THAT COULD POINT TOWARD SICKNESS. IN OUR NEARLY THIRTY YEARS, WE

HAVE NEVER ONCE CONTRACTED ANYTHING FROM OUR PREY. WE CAME TO BELIEVE A LONG TIME AGO THAT WE ARE IMMUNE, BUT WE ARE VIGILANT, NONETHELESS.

WHEN MY EXAMINATION IS FINISHED, I TAKE THE STRAIGHT RAZOR FROM THE TUB'S EDGE AND CAREFULLY SHAVE AWAY ANY STRAY HAIR AROUND HIS COCK THAT SEEMS OUT OF PLACE. THIS IS PART OF OUR IMAGE. WE MUST REFLECT EACH OTHER PERFECTLY. WHEN I'M FINISHED, I RUB LOTION ONTO HIS SKIN TO PREVENT REDNESS BEFORE STANDING. I KISS HIS MOUTH SOFTLY AND SMILE.

"ALL READY."

"YOUR TURN," HE SAYS WITH A SMILE THAT I KNOW IS MY OWN.

WE TRADE PLACES, AND I ADMINISTER THE SAME EXAMINATION. I FIND NOTHING, OF COURSE. WHY WOULD I? I LOOK DOWN AT MY OWN PUBIC HAIR AND UP TO HIS TURNING MY HEAD FROM SIDE TO SIDE AND COMPARING BEFORE SHAVING AWAY A FEW STRAYS AND STANDING.

"READY?"

"YES," HE ANSWERS.

WE EMBRACE AND LET THE WATER RUN OVER US FOR A MOMENT BEFORE I REACH BEHIND HIM AND SWITCH OFF THE HOT. CALEB'S MUSCLE'S TENSE IN THE SUDDENLY FREEZING SPRAY, BUT HE SOON RELAXES AGAINST ME AGAIN. THE COLD WATER IS GOOD FOR THE PORES, KEEPS OUR SKIN YOUNG.

AFTER A FEW MORE SECONDS, I SWITCH OFF THE WATER, AND WE CAREFULLY STEP OUT OF THE SHOWER TO DRY OFF AND DRESS.

WE PULL ON BLACK TANK TOPS, ONE SIZE TOO SMALL. THIS ACCENTUATES OUR LEAN BUILD BUT ALSO SHOWS OFF OUR TONED MUSCLES.

MATCHING BLACK CARGO PANTS NOT ONLY MAKE OUR ASSES LOOK GREAT, BUT THEY'RE NOT "DRESSED UP" ENOUGH TO MAKE THE LOCALS TAKE TOO MUCH NOTICE.

THE PANTS ARE FUNCTIONAL. THE POCKETS ALLOW US TO STORE BLADES, PHONES, AND WHATEVER ELSE WE MIGHT NEED FOR A NIGHT OUT.

I DOT MY FACE WITH MOISTURIZING CREAM AND PASS THE BOTTLE TO CALEB, WHO DOES THE SAME. OUR COLOGNE SMELLS FAINTLY OF APPLES AND MIXES WELL WITH THE SPICE OF OUR BODY WASH. WE WEAR NO DEODORANT. WE LEARNED A LONG TIME AGO THAT OUR NATURAL SCENT IS IRRESISTIBLE TO A CERTAIN KIND OF MAN.

"I'M READY IF YOU ARE," I SAY.

WE STRAP INTO OUR BLACK WORK BOOTS, THE LAST PIECE OF OUR CAMOUFLAGE, AND STAND TO GIVE EACH OTHER A ONCE OVER. I KNOW FROM CONNOR'S SMILE THAT I LOOK THE PART, AND I NOD TO HIM TO SIGNAL THE SAME.

HE SWITCHES OFF THE LAMPS, AND WE STEP OUT INTO THE NIGHT.

SEVEN

First things first, we need something to eat.

According to the GPS, our options are limited. Like every small Texas town, there's a Dairy Queen, and surprisingly there are a couple of other national chains at hand, but there's also a mom-and-pop Italian establishment simply called Bianchi's. The choice is a no-brainer.

Word to the wise, the best Italian food, just the like the best Mexican, Greek, Chinese, or whatever other cultural food you might be looking for, never comes from a chain. You need a one-location hole-in-the-wall that might not even look much like a restaurant if you want authentic. I know we made the right decision as soon as we step through the door.

Particle board tables with chairs just one step above the folding kind dot the dining area. The checkerboard floors are classic, and the pictures on the walls are no doubt family photos from the last century. Only two of the tables are occupied.

"Have a seat wherever you like," someone calls, and we

DO JUST THAT WITHOUT LOOKING FOR THE SOURCE OF THE VOICE.
A TABLE IN THE CORNER SUITS OUR NEEDS. WE LIKE TO WATCH
THE ROOM.

COLORFUL, LAMINATED MENUS SIT IN THE CENTER OF THE
TABLE ALONG WITH A NAPKIN DISPENSER AND SALT, PEPPER,
AND PARMESAN SHAKERS. WE FLIP THE MENUS OPEN AND BEGIN
BROWSING. WE ARE AWARE OF THE WAITER APPROACHING, BUT
WE WAIT UNTIL HE'S AT THE TABLE TO ACKNOWLEDGE HIM.

"Hello, gents," he says. HIS ACCENT IS THICK, AND HE BLUSHES
WHEN WE BOTH SMILE UP AT HIM. "Yo, you're twins."

"WE ARE," I REPLY, HOLDING OUT A HAND TO HIM. "NAME'S
CONNOR. HE'S CALEB. AND YOU ARE?"

"Tonio," he answers.

HE HOPES WE DON'T NOTICE THE LIGHT BLUSH THAT REDDENS
HIS EARS.

"WELL, TONIO, THIS IS OUR FIRST TIME HERE. WHAT DO YOU
RECOMMEND?"

"Everything's good," he says. "All depends on what you like.
My mama opened this place with my dad almost thirty years ago,
right after I was born. The recipes we use are all hers. I teach all
the new chefs when they hire on."

"THAT'S GREAT. ARE YOUR PARENTS STILL …?" I LET THE

SILENCE STRETCH BETWEEN US, AND HE FURROWS HIS FOREHEAD AT ME.

"Oh! Oh yeah, they're still around. They work the day shift now. Never miss a day."

"Excellent."

"I'll have the cannelloni al forno."

"Good choice!"

I wonder if he's always this enthusiastic.

Connor orders the same, and Tonio taps his order book with his pen.

"Drinks?"

"Just water, for now," I tell him. "We're going to get drinks later."

"Where?"

"Where do you recommend?"

"There's not much in the way of bars out here."

"Oh," I said, giving him my best pouty frown.

"Yeah, it's a little too churchy. Doesn't stop the locals from driving to the next town to get their liquor, though. There's a couple of bars about twenty minutes from here."

"WE WERE HOPING TO JUST HAVE A COUPLE AND RELAX."

"MAYBE, WE'LL JUST HEAD BACK TO THE MOTEL INSTEAD," I SAY, EYEING CALEB ACROSS THE TABLE. "MIGHT BE ABLE TO FIND SOMETHING TOMORROW."

MY TWIN NODS. HE NODS IN AGREEMENT.

Tonio watches us.

HIS EYES NEVER LEAVE US. HE TURNS AWAY TO TAKE OUR ORDERS TO THE KITCHEN THEN TURNS BACK.

"You know," he says, leaning forward conspiratorially. "We're actually closing soon. You guys wanna hang out?"

"HERE?"

His grin is sheepish.

"Why not? I've got a full bar."

CALEB STEPS INTO HIS ROLE.

"WON'T YOUR PARENTS MIND?"

"Nah, they won't even know. They're already in bed. Trust me. They show up here at six in the morning to start the sauces every day."

"What do you think, Caleb?"

"I'm game if you are."

I smile up at Tonio and nod. His grin gets even bigger.

"Sweet. I never get to hang out much with anyone. Let me get your food for you. How about those drinks?"

"Bourbon, rocks."

"Wine. Something dry and red."

"You got it," he says and disappears into the kitchen.

* * *

An hour later, the blinds are drawn, the lights are dimmed, and Caleb and I are sitting at the bar while Tonio works the tabs serving up pints of dark beer. The taste is spicy with just a hint of apple.

"You sure you don't want us to help clean up?"

"Nah, it's all good. I'll just clean up before I leave tonight."

I HOLD UP MY GLASS IN A TOAST, AND HE DOES THE SAME.

"THE FOOD WAS GREAT. BEST ITALIAN I'VE HAD IN YEARS," CALEB SAYS, SIPPING HIS BEER.

"I appreciate that. We work hard to keep it authentic."

"IT SHOWS. SO, IS THERE A MRS. TONIO?"

"What?!" Tonio laughs.

"GOOD LOOKING GUY LIKE YOU, I JUST FIGURED —"

"I got close once, but nah, no Mrs."

"HOW ABOUT A MISTER?"

EVEN IN THE DIMMED LIGHT, I CAN SEE TONIO BLUSHING AGAIN.

"Don't have one of those either," he says.

I DON'T PUSH IT. IT'S TOO EARLY.

"SO, WHAT DO YOU DO? BESIDES WORK?"

"What do you mean?"

"YOU'VE GOTTA HAVE A HOBBY OR SOMETHING."

"Oh, I mean, I read a lot. I go camping sometimes."

"WITH FRIENDS?"

HE'S SILENT FOR A MINUTE. "Mom and pop ... they need a lot of help. I've gotta be around."

"THAT'S COOL."

He takes a long draw off his beer.

"THEY WANT YOU TO BE HAPPY, RIGHT? THEY GOTTA WANT GRANDKIDS."

"They do, but –"

"BUT THEY DON'T GIVE YOU ANY TIME TO HAVE A SOCIAL LIFE." HIS SHOULDERS SLUMP. HE LEANS ON THE BAR.

"AND MAYBE ... IT WON'T BE SO EASY FOR YOU TO GIVE THEM GRANDKIDS."

A SINGLE TEAR GLISTENS ON HIS CHEEK.

"DO THEY KNOW?"

HE SHAKES HIS HEAD.

"Pop's old school. He's not ... he doesn't think ...."

"HE'S A HOMOPHOBE."

"No! He just … doesn't understand."

"Our parents were the same way."

I reach across the bar, and grab Tonio's hand. He almost pulls away, but then he squeezes.

Like a lifeline.

Or a fish on a hook.

"Gosh, everything's so serious," I say, pushing away from the bar. I hold out a hand to Tonio, and after a moment, he takes it. "Let's dance."

"There's no music," he protests.

On cue, Connor's phone lights up. Three taps on the screen later, Solomon Burke's voice fills the dining room, singing "Cry to Me."

I lead him away from the bar and slide my arms around his neck. His own strong arms slide around my waist. I hold his gaze with my own as we sway back and forth. He's not a great dancer, but he does things with his hips that give me just a taste of what's to come. As Solomon heads into the first chorus, I lean into him. He smells like sausage and pepperoni and pizza sauce, and somehow, I can't think of anything more perfect.

HE STARTLES WHEN CONNOR WRAPS AN ARM AROUND HIS WAIST FROM BEHIND, BUT ONLY FOR A SECOND.

HE LEANS BACK AGAINST ME, AND I KISS THE SOFT SKIN JUST BENEATH HIS EAR, THEN NIP AT HIS EARLOBE. HE TURNS HIS EYES TOWARD ME, AND THE DESIRE IS WRITTEN IN BIG BLOCK LETTERS ACROSS THE DARK IRISES. I COVER HIS MOUTH WITH MY OWN, AND HE MOANS INTO ME.

"YOU'VE EARNED THIS," I WHISPER INTO HIS EAR. "JUST FEEL, BABY."

HE BREATHES IN DEEP THROUGH HIS NOSE, BREAKING THE KISS TO LOOK AT ME. I UNTUCK HIS T-SHIRT FROM HIS PANTS, REVEALING A FOREST OF DARK HAIR OVER A TIGHT, TONED STOMACH. I BEND DOWN AND KISS THE FLESH, RUNNING MY TONGUE THROUGH THE COARSE HAIR AND DOWN TO THE WAISTLINE OF HIS JEANS. I UNFASTEN THEM, THEN STAND UP. I WANT TO SEE HIS FACE WHEN I SLIP MY HAND DOWN INSIDE THE DENIM. I FEEL THE TUFTS OF COARSE HAIR, SMILING.

OF COURSE, HE KEEPS IT NATURAL.

HE'S LEANING BACK AGAINST CONNOR, LOOKING INTO MY EYES. I HOLD THE GAZE UNTIL HIS EYES ROLL BACK WHEN I WRAP MY HAND AROUND THE THICK SHAFT OF HIS COCK.

IT'S HARD AND DRIPPING ALREADY, AND WHEN THE MUSKY SMELL OF HIM REACHES MY NOSE, I CAN THINK OF NOTHING BUT DEVOURING HIM. INSTEAD, I SLIDE UP HIS BODY AND KISS HIM

DEEPLY, TRAILING MY FINGERS ALONG THE SHAFT, READING THE VEINS LIKE BRAILLE.

I PULL HIS SHIRT UP OVER HIS HEAD, THEN DROP MY OWN ON THE FLOOR. CALEB DOES THE SAME, AND FOR A LONG MOMENT, WE SAVOR THE FEEL OF SKIN ON SKIN.

THEN, I PUSH HIS JEANS DOWN, MARVELING AT THE DARK HAIR ON HIS LEGS. HE'S SO MUCH HAIRIER THAN I EXPECTED, AND I LOVE IT. AS MY HANDS REACH HIS CALVES, CONNOR TIPS HIM BACKWARD. WE LOWER HIM TO THE FLOOR TOGETHER, AND I REMOVE HIS SHOES AND TOSS HIS PANTS AWAY.

I DROP MY OWN PANTS UNCEREMONIOUSLY. MY NEED IS ON THE PRECIPICE OF OVERRIDING MY SENSES, BUT I WRESTLE IT INTO SUBMISSION BEFORE DROPPING BETWEEN THOSE BEAUTIFUL LEGS AND RUNNING MY FINGERS UP THE BACK OF HIS THIGHS.

I DROP TO MY KNEES, LEANING OVER TONIO ON THE FLOOR AND PULLING CALEB TOWARD ME. OUR LOVER TURNS HIS FACE INTO MY THIGH. HE KISSES, LICKS, TASTES, AND TEASES, DRAWING WHATEVER HE CAN REACH INTO HIS MOUTH. I SWEETLY KISS CALEB BEFORE PRESSING HIS ASS DOWN OVER TONIO'S COCK.

THERE'S NO PENETRATION. I ROCK MY ASS BACK AND FORTH ACROSS HIM, FEELING HIS COCK JUMP WITH EVERY MOVE.

I SCOOT FORWARD, SIT ON TONIO'S CHEST AND LOOK BACK AT HIM, GRINNING. HE SEEMS A LITTLE CONFUSED, BUT AROUSAL GLOWS FROM HIS SKIN. THE HAIR ON HIS CHEST TICKLES MY

SKIN. I PUSH MY COCKHEAD DOWN INTO THE SEA OF BLACK HAIR, MOVING BACK AND FORTH, PRECUM OOZING, GLEAMING IN THE DIM LIGHT. HIS STRONG ARMS COME UP BETWEEN MY LEGS, FORCING ME BACK ONTO HIS FACE. HIS TONGUE FINDS WHAT HE'S LOOKING FOR, AND HE PROBES DEEP.

I LEAN FORWARD, PULLING HIS FACE TO MINE. MY COCK GRAZES MY TWIN'S CUM-TRAIL SLICKING MY SKIN AND SENDING FIERY SIGNALS TO MY BRAIN. CONNOR GASPS, RIDING TONIO'S FACE. I REACH BEHIND ME, GRIPPING THE HOODED, UNCUT COCK. LIVING, PULSATING, VEINED STEEL. HE PUSHES INTO MY HAND, AND I STROKE HIM. HIS MUFFLED MOANS ESCAPE FROM BENEATH CONNOR. I STROKE HIM HARDER, FASTER, BENDING FORWARD BEFORE SLIDING MY ASS ONTO HIM FOR REAL THIS TIME. WITH ONLY SWEAT AND HIS OWN PRECUM FOR THE LUBE, THE PAIN IS INSTANT. I SHIVER AND DIG MY NAILS INTO HIS CHEST. HE YELLS, TURNING HIS HEAD FROM HIS MINISTRATIONS TO CONNOR'S ASS. HIS VOICE IS GRUFF; HIS WORDS SLUR AROUND SWOLLEN LIPS AND TONGUE.

"Fuck. Yes. Just like that. Don't stop."

I PUSH UP AND OFF OF TONIO'S CHEST, TURNING AROUND TO FACE HIM. MY PANTS ARE NEXT TO HIS HEAD. I SLIDE DOWN HIS BODY, RUN MY FINGERS THROUGH HIS DARK HAIR AND KISS HIM. I MOAN WITH HIM, INCHING MY FINGERS FORWARD UNTIL I CAN FEEL THE HARD OUTLINE OF THE STRAIGHT RAZOR'S HANDLE THROUGH THE CARGO PANTS. I ROCK FORWARD, OFFERING MY THROAT TO HIM. HE KISSES AND SUCKS, SENDING SHIVERS DOWN MY SPINE.

I FEEL THE WARM WET SPRAY OF CALEB'S CUM ON MY BACK. TONIO'S BACK ARCHES BENEATH ME. AS SMOOTH AND CALCULATED AS A SNAKE READY TO STRIKE, I PUSH UP FROM THE FLOOR, FLICK OPEN THE BLADE, AND DRAW IT ACROSS TONIO'S NECK.

THE FEEL OF TEARING TENDONS AND MUSCLE IS, IN ITS OWN WAY, SEXUAL. TONIO'S BLOOD SPRAYS MY CHEST AND RUNS DOWN TO MY COCK. THERE'S NOTHING MORE AROUSING THAN USING A MAN'S BLOOD AS LUBRICATION. I STROKE MY WET, RED COCK UNTIL I MOAN, SPEWING THICK ROPES OF CUM OVER TONIO'S DEAD FACE.

EIGHT

RYAN SHIFTED ON the hard motel mattress and stared at his phone on the table that separated his bed from Lane's. The man was asleep, and it was only a matter of time before he started moaning again. When he'd woken up screaming the first night after they'd set out on the road together, Ryan had fallen out of his own bed in a panic. Now, after only three days, he'd come to anticipate his sullen travel companion's nightly terrors.

He felt bad for Lane. He knew he was tormented by the scene he'd witnessed when he found his friend dead. During the day, he constantly fidgeted. While driving, his fingers drummed against the wheel as he rocked back and forth to the music, even when the radio wasn't on. At night, he tossed and turned until sleep took him. Then he'd wake, screaming and flailing his arms against attackers only he could see.

Ryan didn't doubt that trauma was real. What he doubted was that the twins he met were the culprits. The men he met were many things. Sexy and seductive, like something out of a taboo story in a dark corner of the internet. He'd never felt the way he had with them. He wanted them, and he'd do whatever he had to do to be with them.

What if they're serial killers?

His mind slipped the questions between his thoughts so smoothly that he winced.

He'd considered it.

Riding across west Texas with Lane, how could he not?

The question gnawed at him, filled his mind in the quiet hours of the night while he waited for Lane to wake up shouting about blood and gore. He knew his answer, but he'd yet to give it to that questioning, logical part of his brain.

If they found them and they weren't guilty, he would apologize for running from them and ask them to take him to bed.

And if they were?

If they were, he'd do the same.

It wasn't like he had a lot to live for. His life hit a dead-end years before, and he'd only been existing ever since. His family would never accept who he really was. They barely tolerated him now, and their violently conservative religious superiority was stifling. He'd never been the son or brother they wanted him to be. He doubted, even now, that they were looking for him after he'd left so abruptly.

He didn't know, of course. He hadn't turned his phone on after that first day, but that part of his brain that had been shaped by their disappointment, molded by every long-suffering sigh, reassured him that he was right.

You could check.

Frowning, he picked up the phone. His finger hovered over the power button as seconds ticked away in the darkened room. Lane grumbled and rolled over, turning his back to him.

Before he could second-guess himself again, Ryan pressed the button.

He flinched as the phone immediately sprang to life, illuminating his face. When it finished booting, the phone vibrated three times in quick succession. Three messages. All of them were from his father. He drew in a deep breath, and again, his finger hovered over the icon.

Rip the bandage.

He tapped and shook his head.

How dare you leave the motel unsupervised?

I always knew you'd do something like this.

Wherever you are, stay there. We don't want or need you here anymore. I'm done.

And that was that.

There were no messages from his mother or brothers. No one knew or cared where he was. Cold hatred filled his chest. He breathed in slowly, then exhaled. To his surprise, the hate disappeared as quickly as it came. It had only been a matter of time, really, before this happened, and in a way, it had happened on his own terms, which was more than he'd expected.

Ryan deleted his father's messages, then deleted and blocked every member of his family from calling him. Social media went next. He didn't have many friends to begin with, and he didn't want his family tracking him down. A clean break. That's what he wanted…needed.

"Fuck you," he muttered as he deleted the icons, one by one, from his phone.

From behind him, he heard more murmuring. It was louder this time. He pushed himself up from the bed, turned, and put both feet on the floor, leaning forward, preparing to wake Lane up at the first scream. Time stretched and slowed.

Any second now.

No scream came.

Instead, there was a small whimper, a choked sob, and the unmistakable sniff of someone crying.

Ryan froze. He wasn't prepared for this. He held his breath, listening to the man he hardly knew weep quietly in his bed, and for the first time in longer than he could remember, tears pricked his own eyes.

On autopilot, he stood up, leaned over the bed, and held out his hand so close he could feel the heat from Lane's body.

"Hey," he whispered. "Lane? Are … are you okay?"

Lane's voice was ragged and torn.

"Leave me alone."

"I just—"

"I said *leave me alone!*"

Lane flipped over in the bed so fast that Ryan simultaneously jumped and stepped to the side to avoid being hit. He tripped hard and fell to the floor, his arm twisting painfully behind him.

"Fuck!"

The younger man rolled to extract his arm from beneath him and scrambled across the floor when he heard the squeak of bedsprings from Lane's side of the bed.

"Hey … hey, I'm sorry. Just … I'm sorry. Are you okay?"

"Stay back!"

Lane froze, holding his hands out in front of him in a truce. Ryan's chest rose and fell in time with his rapid heartbeat. He squeezed his eyes shut and forced himself to breathe deeply, in and out. His breathing calmed, but his heartbeat did not. He looked up at the looming strange with whom he'd be traveling and shook his head.

"I don't think this is a good idea," he said finally.

"What?"

"You, me, this insane road trip to nowhere."

Lane sat on the edge of the bed. He propped his elbows on his knees and rubbed his swollen eyes.

"I know," he admitted finally. "I just … don't know what else to do. I can't go back home. I can't get it all out of my head."

"Not until you've murdered two people."

"They murdered my friend first."

"If you kill them, what comes next?"

The man looked up at him finally. Ryan pushed himself up into a sitting position and chewed the inside of his lip, waiting for an answer.

"I don't know."

"You think it'll make the nightmares end?"

"No."

"It'll make you stop thinking about it?"

"No."

"Then what?"

"I don't know."

"What's really bugging you? The murder or the part where you didn't know your friend liked to have sex with men?"

Lane sucked in a quick, ragged breath. Ryan watched tears well, but they didn't fall. His traveling companion wouldn't cry openly in front of a stranger any more than he would, not if he could help it.

"You wouldn't understand."

Lane waved his hand and turned to lie back down. He made a show of turning to face the wall, pulling the cheap motel comforter up over his shoulders. Ryan pushed himself up from the floor and walked to his own bed. He didn't lie down, though. He sat, watching Lane. When he finally spoke, his voice was hoarse.

"You were best friends. You grew up together, did everything together, and told each other everything. You got in trouble together, took your punishments together. As you got older, you talked about girls, struggled in the same classes, chose the same friends, and found better ways of getting in trouble.

"There was a kid at your school. Maybe a year ahead or behind. Maybe the same age. He wasn't like the other kids at your school, and for nothing more than being himself, you painted a target on his back together. You and Mark and all your friends tormented him. You called him names behind his back and to his face. You took every opportunity to kick him while he was down, which was easy because you never really let him up.

"And all the while, you thought Mark was right there with you. You thought he loved the queer jokes. He always laughed, right? And even if he didn't, not the way you did, he never told you to stop, never said to leave the kid alone, never stuck up for him. He was the same as you. You weren't doing anything wrong. The kid had it coming. That's what being queer earned you in a small town in the middle of nowhere. If he wanted to be like that, he should have gone somewhere else.

"The kicker is, that kid might not even have been queer, but all the while, your best friend was. The guy who laughed with you, stayed up late at night with you, was closer to you than any other person in the whole world had ever been. The guy you told your secrets to was queer. The guy you grew up with liked to fuck guys, and what if, when he was all alone in the closet, when he closed his eyes and dreamed of putting his hands on another man, he was thinking about you. It's possible. Hell, it's probable.

"But you'll never know because all that time you were making jokes and treating that kid like shit, you were telling him everything he needed to know about you and what you thought about queerness. And he laughed and went along because it was safe, which makes him human but maybe a coward, too."

He knew Lane was listening when his shoulders stiffened at the word "coward." That's all right. He was almost done.

"A part of you hasn't been able to let that go since Mark died. You think about it constantly while you drive, tapping your fingers on the steering wheel. You think that maybe if he'd just been honest with you, things might have been different. At the very least, he wouldn't have necessarily been picking strangers up in a bar. The way I figure it, you're trying to decide how much of it is your fault, and finding his killers, killing them... well, that's the only way you can make it up to him."

Ryan pulled his own scratchy comforter up to his shoulders, shifted down in the bed, and turned his back on Lane.

"Mark and I have a lot in common," he said. "The only real difference is no one's killed me ... yet."

Ryan closed his eyes and pulled his pillow up over his exposed ear to muffle the sobs from the other side of the room.

NINE

THE SUN HAD barely broken over the horizon the following morning when Lane's phone began buzzing on the nightstand. He rolled over, bleary-eyed, and picked it up, repeatedly blinking until the screen came into focus.

JESSICA

His thumb hovered over the screen. He should answer. He owed that much to her.

But he couldn't.

He tapped the screen, sending the call to voicemail, and fell back onto the pillow, staring up at the ceiling. He heard Ryan stir the other bed and sighed.

"Sebastian Kessler."

The two words hung in the air above him. He knew by the sudden stillness that Ryan heard him, knew he was listening.

"That was the kid's name. He was always clean, made good grades, and wasn't interested in sports. Plus, his name was Sebastian, and damn it, I know he didn't have anything to do with it, but it just wasn't a ... *normal* name."

Lane rolled over to find Ryan staring at him. His face was pale, and he looked so damned young.

"Sebastian's married, now ... to a woman. They've got eight kids. Couple years back, we had our high school reunion. Mark and I apologized to him. Mark ... it was his idea. He said we owed it to the man. Said we were stupid—which I couldn't argue with—and that it was time to make things right. There was something about the way he said it. I couldn't put my finger on it, but it wasn't guilt. Or it wasn't only guilt.

"Look, you weren't completely wrong, but you weren't completely right either."

The younger man raised an eyebrow at him, and Lane sighed, pushing himself up in bed. Ryan stayed where he was, but his eyes followed the other man's movements. Lane fought the urge to cover himself up. He'd never been looked at by a man like that.

Well, only once.

"In high school, I was a walking hormone. I mean, I know most teenage boys are, but I was seriously a walking boner. So, this one time, I swiped a porn mag from a convenience store and took it over to Mark's place. We went out to this shed he had in the back of his house and were looking through it. I'm not sure how it happened; not sure who pulled their dick out first. Doesn't matter, really. We were teenagers with big libidos, and no one else was around.

"So, there we are, stroking. I remember at some point realizing Mark wasn't looking at the magazine anymore. He was looking at me. I turned my head, met his eyes, and my breath caught. The look … it was so intense. We'd both pulled our shirts off, and our shoulders were just barely touching. Mark was right-handed and sitting on my left. It only took a second to realize the movements I felt, the graze of his skin on mine, was timed with his strokes."

Ryan shifted under the covers, but he didn't say anything. Lane wondered if he was turned on by the story, but he wouldn't ask. He didn't want to know.

Did he?

"I only looked down once. A bead of sweat ran down the side of Mark's face … onto his neck … down onto his chest. I followed it with my eyes until it disappeared. Then I looked down. Mark's dick was thicker than mine, and the hair around the base looked so soft. I watched his steady stroke and saw the head fatten up. I knew it wouldn't be long before he shot his load.

"When I looked him in the eyes again, he was … so close. He was moaning quietly, and I realized I was too. He quickened his pace, and I timed mine to his. That little patch of skin where we were touching was on fire, like everything I was feeling, and he was feeling all sat right there. I thought it might catch fire, but it didn't. Then Mark shot his load. It wasn't loud. He didn't shout. It wasn't like porn. It was so real, so strong. When a splash of cum hit his chin, I wanted to lick it off. I wanted to taste him, and the thought of it pushed me over the edge.

"I filled my own hand. The jizz ran over my fingers and down into my pubic hair, slick and slimy and pungent. He never looked away. Neither did I. We just stared at each other, and then he leaned toward me until his forehead touched my shoulder. We sat there like that until we were breathing normally. Mark got up, tossed me a shop towel to clean up with, and we never talked about it again."

Lane looked at Ryan. Ryan looked at Lane.

Ryan said nothing. Lane pushed himself up off the bed. His light grey sweatpants hung loosely around his hips but not so loose that they hid the outline of his semi-erect cock. He opened his mouth like he might say something but realized he didn't know what to say. He shrugged and stepped into the tiny motel bathroom, turned the water on as hot as he could stand it, and stepped under the spray.

His mind wandered again back to that day with Mark in the old shed. He thought about the look in Mark's eyes, tried to decipher the meaning of a decades-old puzzle that hadn't seemed relevant until Mark was killed. Tears threatened again, and he turned his face up to the shower head, letting the hot water wash away salty regret.

Lane considered himself as he ran the cheap motel bar soap over his skin. Ryan said a lot of shit the night before that made sense. Some of what he said was so on the nose he would have sworn the younger man was psychic. But there was one thing he missed. One thing he wasn't entirely right or wrong about. It was true he thought about Mark constantly as they drove up and down the highway looking for the twins. It was true he wondered if Mark had ever thought about telling him, that maybe it was somehow his fault his friend had never opened up to him.

What Ryan missed is that sometimes, when he was alone and horny, it was Mark he thought of when he rubbed one out. That bead of sweat trickling down his best friend's skin, the look in his eyes, the droplets of cum on his chin. He'd whispered Mark's name so many times over the years at the moment of orgasm that he often worried it might slip out when he was with someone else. When he was with Jessica.

He wouldn't call himself gay. Hell, he wouldn't even call himself bisexual. He didn't know what you called fantasizing about one man and only one man in your lifetime. There probably wasn't a name for it, and that made him feel alone.

Lane stepped under the spray and let the hot water wash away the soap, running his hands over the coarse hair on his chest and stomach, then slipped it lower, scrubbing around his cock and balls. He let out a low sigh, then jumped when the door to the bathroom creaked open. He slipped, nearly falling, then stuck his head out from behind the shower curtain.

"What the fuck?"

"Sorry. Just needed my brush."

Ryan looked him in the eyes. Lane stared back and, for a moment, considered holding a hand out to him. He didn't know what he'd do if the man accepted, but he wanted to. Maybe things would make sense then. Maybe he'd be even more confused than before. Either way, he said nothing. Instead, he pulled the curtain back and listened intently for the door to latch before finishing his shower.

When he emerged from the bathroom with a towel tightly wrapped around him, Ryan was staring at the screen of his phone. The younger man didn't immediately acknowledge him, which gave him time to fish his last pair of clean jeans out of his duffel bag and slip them on before dropping the towel with his back to him. When he turned, Ryan was looking up at him, holding out his phone.

Lane took the phone and sat down on the edge of his bed to read:

> MURDER IN A SMALL TOWN
> Authorities are baffled at the violent murder of Borger resident Antonio Bianchi. The son of local restauranteurs was found in the family's business. His throat had apparently been cut. Bianchi closed the restaurant for his parents as he usually did when he was allegedly attacked.

A local couple who were some of the last customers in the establishment that evening says nothing seemed out of the ordinary, although they did remember seeing a pair of young men chatting with Bianchi throughout the evening. While it has not been confirmed, the witnesses reportedly mentioned the two men might have been twins.

There was more, but Lane stopped reading. Emotions raged inside him. His vision tunneled, and he thought, for a moment, that he might vomit. It was them. He knew it was them. Deep down in his gut, he was sure. He grabbed his own phone and tapped on the GPS app, typing in Borger.

"Shit," he whispered. "We've been going in the wrong direction. Fuck. Get dressed."

"What?"

"Get dressed. We're leaving in ten minutes. Get your shit together."

Ryan looked at him like he might protest but reconsidered. He grabbed his bag and began shoving his things into it. In eight minutes, they were in the truck and on the road. He grabbed the "shit handle" over the passenger window and held on for dear life as Lane took corners driving far too fast, and wondered if they'd live to find the twins.

TEN

"Hi, mom."

MY VOICE IS BRIGHT AND HAPPY AS I ANSWER, TAPPING THE SPEAKER BUTTON SO WE CAN BOTH HEAR. IT'S BEEN A WHILE SINCE SHE CALLED US.

"HEY, MOM."

"How are my boys?"

"WE'RE GOOD, ON THE ROAD."

"I know," she says, and her voice is suddenly tense.

"SOMETHING WRONG?"

"What? No, of course not. Why would something be wrong?"

I OPEN MY MOUTH TO ANSWER, BUT SHE CUTS ME OFF.

"I was just scrolling through the news on my phone, and I saw that a young man was murdered over in Borger. They're saying a couple of twins were in the restaurant before the murder."

"Oh? That's sad. I wonder what happened?"

"You two wouldn't know anything about that, would you?"

"Mom, you're getting paranoid again. Have you been taking your pills?"

"Caleb Martin Chapelwaite, don't you take that tone with me."

I flinch at the use of my full name.

"Calm down, mom. You're getting worked up over nothing." *As usual,* hangs in the air unsaid.

She has long suspected our nature.

She never says anything, but after Alvin, our very first, she always looked at us like she was trying to figure out how to ask without asking.

We consider cutting ties with her over it, but she's our mother, even if she thinks we're monsters.

We are not monsters.

Of course, we're not. We are human.

Humans raised to the power of humans. We don't deny our natures. We lean into them.

"I don't know what to do with you boys."

"YOU NEVER HAVE."

"NEVER WILL."

"I have half a mind to call the police."

CALEB TRIES TO GRAB THE PHONE, BUT I HOLD IT OUT OF REACH.

"REALLY? WHAT WILL YOU TELL THEM?"

SILENCE.

Then, "You have to stop this."

"STOP WHAT?"

"You know what."

"MOM, IS DAD HOME?"

"NO...."

"HOW MUCH CHARDONNAY HAVE YOU HAD TODAY, MOM?"

"That's none of your god-damned business."

"EXACTLY," I AGREE. "AND WHAT CALEB AND I DO OR DON'T DO
IS NONE OF YOURS."

"I don't understand," she says. Her voice fills with the crocodile tears we've witnessed our entire lives.

PURE PASSIVE-AGGRESSIVE MANIPULATION IN THE WAY SOUTHERN MOTHERS EXCEL. IT'S NEVER REALLY WORKED ON US, BUT SHE NEVER STOPS TRYING.

"WHAT'S TO UNDERSTAND? WHEN WAS THE LAST TIME WE SAW YOU? I BET YOU DON'T EVEN REMEMBER."

"Six years, fourth months, and seventeen days ago."

I LOOK TO CONNOR, WHOSE EYES ARE WIDE. WE ARE RARELY CAUGHT OFF GUARD, ESPECIALLY BY HER. I RECOVER QUICKLY. "AND AFTER ALL THIS TIME, YOU DECIDE YOU WANT TO UNDERSTAND?"

"Baby, I've wanted to understand your whole lives."

HER VOICE IS TENSE, STRAINED. I ALMOST THINK FOR A MOMENT SHE'S BEING GENUINE. THEN I HEAR THE POP OF A CORK FORCIBLY PULLED FROM THE BOTTLE AND ROLL MY EYES. SHE CONTINUES, AND IT'S LIKE SHE'S TALKING TO HERSELF.

"I was so happy when you were born. We knew twins were going to be a handful, but honestly, your dad and I thought we were up to the challenge. It took so long for us to conceive. I wasn't going to complain about two babies for the price of one."

We're both silent. We've never heard this before.

"You were too quiet. I noticed that from the beginning. Your dad told me I ought to be thankful you weren't crying all the time, but it just wasn't natural. The only time you ever got angry was when I tried to separate the two of you. God forbid only one of you shit yourself at a time. The other would scream their head off until I finished changing you. It got so I wouldn't do anything for just one of you. If one of you was hungry, you both ate. If one of you was tired, you both slept. If one of you was in trouble, I'd use the belt on both of you."

I frowned. This, I do remember. I remember her rages when she'd suddenly burst into our rooms, belt swinging from her hand. Most of the time, neither of us knew what she was so angry about. Eventually, we decided she was hurting us because she didn't know what else to do.

She was already putting back a lot of wine by the time we were seven or eight. Some people have sense memories of their mother's perfume. Ours are chardonnay and white zinfandel.

We'd come home from school to find her sleeping on the couch with dinner burning on the stove.

Sit through slurred conversations at dinner.

Hear her arguing with dad late at night.

GLASS BREAKING AND THE SOUNDS OF HER HITTING HIM WHEN HE WOULDN'T ARGUE ANYMORE.

THEN, THE NEXT MORNING SHE'D ACT LIKE NOTHING HAPPENED, SERVING PANCAKES FOR BREAKFAST.

SOME FOLKS WOULD SEE THIS AND POINT OUT THAT THIS IS WHY WE ARE THE WAY WE ARE.

AND THEY'D BE WRONG. WE DO WHAT WE DO BECAUSE WE LIKE IT. WE KILL BECAUSE IT MAKES US HAPPY, CONNECTS US IN THE ONLY WAY THAT REALLY MATTERS.

WE KILL *DESPITE* OUR UPBRINGING, NOT BECAUSE OF IT.

"Are you listening to me?!"

"YES, MOTHER."

"Don't call me that!"

"ALL RIGHT, DIANE. WHY DID YOU CALL?"

"I called because I know you did it. I know you killed that boy. I know you did it together, and God knows what else you did before."

"IS THAT ALL?"

I CAN HEAR HER BLOOD BOILING ON THE PHONE.

I look at Caleb and hold out my hand for the phone. He sighs and hands it to me.

"Mom, where's dad?"

"He's at his office where he always is. He doesn't care. He doesn't even listen to me anymore."

I bite the inside of my lip, look at Connor, and he nods his head.

"Okay, mother, it was us. We killed him, but before we killed him, we fucked him, and it was good. His cock was nice and thick, and according to Connor, the man really knew how to use his tongue. Antonio, that was his name. Antonio Bianchi. He was handsome and kind and sad and lonely. If we hadn't come along, he would have continued to be sad and lonely. Instead, we gave him the fuck of his life, and at the moment, the very second he had an orgasm, Connor slit his throat. Antonio died in ecstasy, mom. We should all be so lucky."

"I ... Caleb ...."

"See, you're upset now because you thought we might have done something but thinking and knowing are two different things. He's not the first, and he won't be the last. Alvin was the first, but somewhere deep down, you knew that. Would you like to know the names of the others, mother? Excuse me, Diane. Would you like to

KNOW ABOUT MARK? DAVID? BENJAMIN? SOL? WOULD YOU LIKE
TO HEAR ALL THEIR STORIES?"

"Stop this! Stop this right now or –"

"OR WHAT? YOU'LL CALL THE POLICE? IT'S A BIT LATE FOR THAT,
DON'T YOU THINK? YOU COULD HAVE STOPPED US A LONG TIME
AGO, MAYBE, BUT WE'RE VERY GOOD AT WHAT WE DO, DIANE.
WE'RE GOOD AT IT, AND WE LIKE IT. DO YOU KNOW WHAT IT'S
LIKE TO HOLD THE LIFE OF ANOTHER PERSON IN YOUR HAND? TO
MAKE THE DECISION TO END IT? YOU TOLD STORIES ALL OUR LIVES
ABOUT HOW WE WERE TOO QUIET AS CHILDREN. HOW WE WERE
CONSTANTLY WHISPERING TO EACH OTHER. PLOTTING. THAT'S
WHAT YOU CALLED IT. DID YOU THINK ABOUT IT, THEN? DID YOU
CONSIDER WE MIGHT HAVE AN ACCIDENT SO YOU COULD PLAY THE
GRIEVING MOTHER?"

"DID YOU DREAM OF THE ATTENTION?"

"I never –"

"HAD THE GUTS TO DO IT. I'VE WONDERED OVER THE YEARS WHY
CALEB AND I WERE CHOSEN. WHY WE WERE GIFTED WITH THIS
DESIRE TO REAP. PERHAPS IT WAS SOMETHING IN THE DRUGS YOU
TOOK WHEN YOU WERE TRYING TO GET PREGNANT."

"Don't you blame me!"

"I'M NOT BLAMING YOU, MOTHER. IF ANYTHING, I'D THANK YOU
IF I THOUGHT IT WAS TRUE. IT WOULD BE THE ONE THING YOU
ABSOLUTELY DID RIGHT BY US. WHEN CALEB AND I LIE TOGETHER

IN BED, NAKED AND COVERED IN ANOTHER MAN'S BLOOD, WE SOMETIMES PRETEND WE'RE BACK IN THE WOMB."

"WE KNEW THE FIRST TIME WE DID IT THAT IT WAS RIGHT ... POWERFUL."

"WHEN IT'S DARK OUTSIDE, AND WE FOCUS ON OUR HEARTBEATS UNTIL THEY SYNC UP, WE WHISPER TO EACH OTHER, THINK ABOUT HOW WE GOT SO LUCKY WHEN OUR PARENTS ARE SUCH FUCKING DISAPPOINTMENTS."

A SOB SCREECHES FROM THE PHONE, AND I ROLL MY EYES.

"I'm going to call the police! They can track your phone. I know they can. I've seen it on TV. They'll catch you and put you in prison for good!"

I SIGH.

"GOODBYE, DIANE."

I HAND THE PHONE BACK TO CALEB. HE ROLLS DOWN THE WINDOW AND THROWS THE PHONE OUT UNCEREMONIOUSLY. THERE'S A LOUD CLANG AS IT BOUNCES OFF A SIGN THAT READS: MULESHOE 20 MILES.

THAT'S AS GOOD A PLACE TO STOP AS ANY.

ELEVEN

LANE PULLED INTO the Economy Inn & Suites in Muleshoe as the sun was going down. He was tired. With the exception of two stops for gas and to take a piss, he had been driving all day. He'd considered letting Ryan drive at one point, but he still wasn't sure he could trust the younger man. He did allow him to go inside and book the room, taking the time to walk around the truck and stretch his ride-weary muscles. When Ryan reemerged, he pointed toward the end of the row of rooms, choosing to walk rather than ride himself.

Lane shook his head, got back in the truck, and crept through the parking lot to park in front of the door where Ryan stopped. He grabbed both their bags and followed him into the darkened room, switching on the bedside lamp and collapsing onto the bed. The motel room was just like any other they'd shared over the last few days. Two somewhat comfortable beds, shower, coffee maker, television, and lamps. Lane knew if he opened the table separating the beds, he'd find a Bible just in case anyone decided a dingy hotel room was the place to get right with the Lord.

The only thing that stood out was the door next to the TV stand that led to an adjoining room. A glance told him that the latch was in place, but it still made him nervous. He didn't like the idea of someone being able to walk into their room.

"It was the cheapest room they had," Ryan said, reading his expression if not his mind. "Someone's already rented the other room. I got a deal."

"Okay," Lane said, rolling onto his back and putting his hands behind his head.

"I'm going to shower," the other man announced, rising from his bed. "You didn't give me time this morning."

Lane didn't imagine the resentment in the tone, and for the first time in a while, he felt bad for being an asshole.

"Sorry," he said. He pushed himself up and grabbed Ryan's wrist when he shrugged and turned away. "Seriously, I know I've not been the easiest guy to get along with. I'm sorry. I just –"

"I know," Ryan said. His smile was sad. "I'll feel better after a shower."

"Okay. You mind if I take a nap?"

"Be my guest," Ryan said, turning again and stepping into the bathroom.

Lane lay back on the bed and stared at the ceiling. They'd made good time today. He was good with that. They didn't talk much, and when they did, it was still uncomfortable. Inside his pocket, his phone buzzed. He groaned and retried it, frowning at Jessica's name. He might as well get this over with while Ryan was out of the way.

"Hello?"

"You sonofabitch."

"Nice to talk to you, too."

"Where the hell are you?"

He thought about telling her, then decided vague was better.

"West Texas."

"West Texas." She said it with a finality that made him wince. "I'm moving out."

He paused. Considered.

"Okay."

"Okay? That's all you've got to say to me?"

"Yeah, it is."

"What the hell are you doing? Driving around in circles by yourself playing detective?"

"No."

"Well?"

"Well, for starters, I'm not alone. Picked up a guy who might be able to identify Mark's killers if we can find them."

"Might. If. You know that's stupid, right?"

"Better than sitting at home acting like it didn't happen."

"Oh, fuck you, Lane. You know what happened to Mark tore me up."

He did, in fact, know that. He'd been the one to break the news to her, had held her while she cried it out. He'd sat next to her at the funeral while folks stared daggers at them. Then, when they got the news back about *how* Mark died, she just up and quit mourning. It was like he hadn't even existed to her, or at best, he was a bad memory she didn't care to dwell on.

When he told her he was going out to find the men who killed Mark, she'd been upset, but she hadn't tried to stop him. He figured she thought he'd be gone a few days and come back. Now, here he was, a couple of months gone, and though he might be getting closer, he didn't have much to show for his time away.

"Listen," he said. "I don't blame you for leaving. I as good as ran out on you. You take what's yours and head out. I have no idea when I'll be home, and it's not fair to ask you to stick around waiting."

Jessica was silent. He figured she'd expected him to apologize, to say he would come home. She was counting on her threat of leaving to snap him out of whatever this was. So, he waited.

"You're a real bastard, Lane," she whispered. "I can't believe you'd choose him over me."

"I'm —"

"Don't lie. Don't make it worse."

"Okay."

"I hope you find them. I hope you do what you gotta do, and I hope you never come back. If I don't see you, I can pretend all this meant something."

"Do you want to know? If I find them?"

He heard her breath catch on the other side of the line, and he laid back on the bed, staring up at the ceiling.

"No," she said finally and ended the call.

He sighed and rolled over, tossing the phone onto the table. He wondered why she didn't ask about Ryan but then supposed it meant she really was done with him and the whole mess. He closed his eyes and, in no time at all, fell into a deep sleep.

* * *

LANE DIDN'T EVEN look up when Ryan emerged from the shower, and the younger man stopped for a minute, looking down at him. He really was handsome. Dark stubble ran along his jaw and chin with glimmers of red here and there. His arms were defined, as were his chest and stomach, which were also dusted with that same dark hair. He sat on the edge of the bed across from Lane and watched him for a while, taking in the measure of him.

A few strands of hair fell over the man's forehead, and without thinking, Ryan gently pushed them away. A warm tug ran through his belly, the same he'd felt when Lane had told him about jerking off with Mark.

He tried to imagine this man sitting on the floor of a dusty shed, sweat dripping down his forehead as he stroked and tugged at himself. He imagined slipping his hand over Lane's, stroking him together.

The fantasy was almost completely painted in his head when Lane suddenly snored and rolled over, turning from him. Ryan nearly fell off the bed, and he decided it was best if he got out of the room for a while before he did something he couldn't take back. He pulled on clothes that were badly in need of washing and stepped out into the twilight.

He didn't see Lane's eyes open, watching him, didn't see the confused expression on his face, which was just as well.

The evening was warm, but there wasn't much humidity. He walked across the parking lot and, when he reached its edge, looked both ways. The motel was on the edge of town. To his right, the highway stretched toward another town much the same as the one he was standing in, and beyond that, there was another and another beyond that one.

To his left, he saw gas stations, a grocery store, and the illuminated sign on a Dairy Queen not so far away. His stomach growled at the sight, and he headed in that direction. He would get food for himself and Lane. He hoped that might ease the tension of the last twenty-four hours. The building was lit up with bright fluorescent lights that were far more welcoming than they should have been.

He ordered Belt Busters with cheese, fries, and sodas, then sat down to wait.

Out the window, evening traffic moved at a pace that was only acceptable in a small town. Folks weren't in a hurry. They had nowhere to be really except home. Across the street, at a little gas station, someone caught his eye. He was tall with wavy dark hair, and he carried himself like he was the most important person in the lot.

Ryan was out of his seat so fast; he nearly fell to the floor. He yelled over his shoulder he'd be right back as he pushed his way into the lot, cursing at the vehicles driving by that obscured his view of the gas station. It was one of them. He knew it. He wanted to yell out to them, then realized he didn't know what he'd say if they saw him.

How would he explain his presence? Would he tell them about Lane? Would he warn them? Would he just ask if they'd give him a ride?

Surely, they'd remember him.

Right?

Right?!

By the time the cars had moved on, no one was in the gas station. Ryan's shoulders fell, and he walked back into the Dairy Queen to find his food was bagged and waiting. He thanked the woman at the counter, took the bags, and walked back out into the night.

TWELVE

"Connor? Look."

"Look at what?"

I turn to him with a grin.

"Come and see."

I push myself off the edge of the bed where I'm flipping channels and join Caleb, who is peeking into the parking lot from behind the burnt orange curtains. At first, I don't see what the fuss is about.

Then.

"Well, I'll be damned."

"It's him, isn't it?"

"Looks like it, but how?"

"Coincidence?"

"No such thing."

"That's a lot of food for one person. You think he's on a date?"

"At a cheap motel in the middle of nowhere? That's basically where he works. Who goes where they work for a date?"

"Anyone who works in a restaurant."

Connor smiles and nudges me with his shoulder.

We watch Ryan a little flummoxed. We've never run into one of our almost playmates a second time.

"To be fair, there have only been three …."

"That's true also. What should we do?"

"Close the curtains. He got away. Those are the rules." I sit and watch him make his way to the room at the end of the row. He opens the door and disappears from view. I am … disappointed? Ryan feels like a loose end that needs to be tied. We don't believe in coincidences. There is a reason he is here, and though Connor pretends he doesn't care, I know it's a lie.

"So, what should we do tonight?"

"I SAW A PIZZA PLACE ON THE WAY INTO TOWN. LET'S SEE IF THEY
DELIVER. I'M TIRED."

I SMILE AND SLIDE ONTO THE BED NEXT TO HIM.

"ALL RIGHT," I SAY. "MAYBE THE DELIVERY BOY WILL BE CUTE."

* * *

LANE WAS LYING on the bed, staring at the television, when Ryan returned to the room.

"Dinner," the younger man said. "Figured we could both do with some hot food. Didn't know what you like on your burgers, so I got all the veggies and sauce on the side."

Lane immediately sat up. His stomach growled, and his mouth watered at the smell of burgers and fries.

"Appreciate it," he said, nodding at the food and drinks. He crossed his legs in the center of the bed and took the offered food and soda. Ryan watched him pick off the onions and tomatoes, leaving the lettuce and pickles in place before spreading ketchup on the bun.

Ryan settled onto his own bed, eating quietly and looking up at the television. Lane had turned on one of those crime procedurals where every case is solved in an hour after the police finally find the one piece of evidence that links the criminal to the crime. He wondered if Lane liked these shows in general or if he was trying to improve his investigation game.

His mind wandered to the gas station and the man getting into the car there. The likelihood of it actually being one of the twins was absurd, but so was the fact that he was riding around in circles looking for them. Maybe, for once, the stars lined up in his favor. He wondered if they were just passing through. Maybe they stopped for the night. Maybe they were in this motel?

What if they were on the other side of the door to the adjoining room?

It was too many ifs and maybes for his liking. He tried to concentrate on the television instead. The detectives were closing in on the murderer. It was dark, and they were chasing the man through a parking garage. As he ran, the killer taunted them, yelling and calling them names. His voice echoed off the structure, confusing his pursuers. Then, of course, he made a mistake, setting off a car alarm. The detectives ran for the vehicle's flashing lights and honked the horn to –

"Shit!"

Startled, Ryan looked over to see Lane holding the lid from his large soda. The cup had fallen away, spilling the drink all over the bed. Ryan immediately grabbed napkins and jumped to help, but it was too late. The loose-knit fabric hadn't so much absorbed the liquid as it had allowed it to pass through to the sheets and mattress underneath. Ryan grabbed the cup and began scooping up the ice so he could throw it into the sink. Lane, meanwhile, jumped up and stripped off his now-wet sweatpants and boxer briefs. Ryan watched him dig through his bag for a moment before he threw his hands up.

"We've gotta find someplace to do laundry tomorrow. I'm out of clean shorts."

"Yeah," Ryan said, trying not to stare at the other man's ass. "I'm in the same boat."

Lane sat down hard, pulling his knees up to his chest and wrapping his arms around them.

"Guess I'm freeballing tonight."

The ridiculousness of their situation fell on Ryan like a ton of bricks, and he began to laugh, long and loud. At first, Lane stared at him like he'd lost his mind, but soon the man's rough veneer began to crack. A grin slowly spread across his face, and he really began to laugh. Ryan could almost see it bubble up from the man's belly, rippling through tense muscles, relaxing them until great open guffaws spilled out of him.

Ryan sat back down on his bed, then slipped onto the floor next to Lane. They laughed until tears rolled down their faces, sitting so close that their shoulders grazed each other. Lane turned to look at him, still grinning. Then, he leaned forward and kissed Ryan on the mouth.

The kiss was gentle and sweet, the way a first kiss should be. Lips softly touching, modulated pressure so as not to be forceful. They pressed, held, then pulled back. Lane's eyes asked the question, and Ryan nodded in response.

The second kiss was hungry, filled with need. Ryan pressed himself to Lane's body when the man put his arm around his waist. He ran his fingers through the coarse dark hair on Lane's chest and down onto his stomach. The muscles flexed under his fingers, hardened. When Lane's tongue pressed to his lips, he opened them eagerly, welcoming the tongue that pressed against his own. The kiss deepened until he thought he might pass out, finally breaking away, turning his head to offer his neck to Lane.

The man's stubble reddened his skin and sent electric shocks to his already throbbing cock. He wanted this man, though he wasn't sure why. When Lane's rough hand slipped beneath his shirt, he was sure he'd be scalded by the heat. Instead of crying out, he moaned an incoherent plea for more and was answered with a rough tug and twist that made his eyes roll back in his head.

"Bed," he whispered. "Up."

"Mmmm," Lane responded.

Ryan grabbed onto the comforter, pulling himself to his feet for a scarce moment. He ripped at his clothes, tossing them away before pushing himself back on the mattress. Lane stood there, cock hard and heavy, pointed toward the floor. His face, though. He looked unsure, and Ryan understood.

"If you don't want to –"

"I ... don't know. I've never."

"I know."

The younger man's heart thumped against his chest, and he realized he wasn't sure how he'd feel if Lane wanted to stop. He would understand, but the sliver of ice that formed in his ribs felt like the beginnings of rejection.

"Can I?"

Lane pointed to the bed, and Ryan nodded, scooting over. His cock was hard and pointing out in front of him, and though it was painful, he pushed it down between his legs for the moment. Lane shook his head and pointed.

"It's okay. You don't have to do that."

"I know," Ryan replied.

The man slid onto the bed with him and slipped that rough hand around Ryan's waist, pulling him close.

"I want this," he said. "I want you. I just ... don't know what that means."

"What do you want it to mean?"

"I don't know that either. Other than Mark, I've never thought about another man before, but ever since last night. Ever since you said what you said, it's all I can think about."

Lane's eyes were soft and deep. Ryan's throat closed around an unexpected lump. He nodded to the older man.

"It doesn't have to mean anything," he whispered as he ran his fingers through Lane's hair, pushing it away from his face. "You're so focused on cause and effect, asking how and why. You forget that sometimes there are no answers. You forget that sometimes needing something – wanting something – is enough."

Ryan wiped away the solitary tear that fell from Lane's eye and smiled at the blush that followed.

"How old are you?" Lane asked.

"Twenty-five."

"You're awful fucking smart for a twenty-five-year-old." Ryan shrugged, and he sighed. "Would it be all right if I just held you for a while?"

Ryan shook his head.

"No," he said, "but if you let me, I'll hold you."

Lane considered, then nodded. He turned over and breathed in deeply when Ryan's arm slipped over him. The younger man curved his body into the other man's, and they exhaled together. In moments, they were asleep.

* * *

PIZZA DELIVERY IS A BUST. THE WOMAN WHO DELIVERED WAS, WELL, A WOMAN. IT'S MIDNIGHT, AND I'M BORED.

AND A BIT PETULANT.

THAT, TOO.

105

"It won't hurt to take a look. I'm just curious how and why he's here."

"It's against the rules."

"Most things we do are against someone's rules. We can bend our own occasionally."

Connor frowns, but he agrees after a few moments.

We step outside and creep quietly to the last room in the row. The lights are out. The television is off. If anyone is inside, they're asleep. Caleb nudges me and hands over the lock-picking kit we keep on hand. I'm not sure this is a good idea, but I'll admit, my curiosity is also piqued.

This motel still uses regular door keys, not upgraded cards. It takes only a couple of minutes to unlock the door and slip inside. The orange-tinted glow of the parking lot lights filters into the room, not bright enough to wake the two sleeping men on the bed farthest from the door.

Tiptoeing across the floor, it doesn't take long to identify Ryan, even with his face buried in the back of the man in front of him. They're naked and uncovered, and honestly, it's quite sexy.

There's something very sweet about it. I drop to my knees to examine the bags at the end of the bed while Connor keeps his eyes locked on the two men.

THE FIRST BAG I OPEN IS RYAN'S. IT'S FILLED WITH AN ODD ASSORTMENT OF SOCKS AND UNDERWEAR AND A FEW SHIRTS AND JEANS. IT LOOKS LIKE IT WAS PACKED IN A HURRY.

A PAIR OF JEANS LAY ACROSS THE SECOND BAG. THERE IS A WALLET IN THE BACK POCKET. I PULL IT OUT AND WALK TO THE LIGHT TO LOOK AT THE DRIVER'S LICENSE. I MAKE A NOTE OF THE NAME BEFORE FLIPPING THROUGH THE SMALL SLEEP OF PHOTOS. IT'S ODD BECAUSE YOU HARDLY SEE THOSE ANYMORE. THERE'S NOT MUCH TO SEE, AND I'M JUST ABOUT TO GO BACK TO THE JEANS WHEN I FREEZE ON THE LAST PHOTO.

MY HEART THUMPS LOUDLY ONCE IN MY CHEST.

CONNOR IS AT MY SIDE IN AN INSTANT.

THE PICTURE SHOWS TWO MEN STANDING IN FRONT OF A LAKE, DRESSED IN JEAN SHORTS AND T-SHIRTS. EACH HOLDS UP A LINE WITH SEVERAL FISH HANGING FROM IT. THE FIRST MAN IS IN BED BEHIND US, BUT THE OTHER.

THE OTHER IS MARK.

WE BOTH TURN TO LOOK BACK AT THE BED. MY FIRST INSTINCT IS TO KILL THEM BOTH, BUT CALEB PUTS HIS HAND ON MY ARM. HIS GRIN IS FILLED WITH MISCHIEF, AND AFTER A MOMENT, MINE MIRRORS HIS.

I SLIP BACK INTO THE JEANS AND REPLACE THE WALLET. I TAKE CONNOR'S HAND, AND WE STEP OUTSIDE, PULLING THE DOOR

QUIETLY SHUT.

WE RETURN TO OUR ROOM AND CLOSE THE DOOR AFTER PUTTING THE DO NOT DISTURB SIGN ON THE HANDLE.

WE HAVE PLANNING TO DO.

THIRTEEN

LANE'S EYES SLOWLY opened as the morning sunlight fell across his face. Ryan's arm still clung to him tightly, and he smiled at its weighted protection. He'd slept through the night without a single nightmare for the first time since discovering Mark's body. For the first time in months, he felt as though he'd actually rested. As gently as he could, he shifted just enough so that he could touch the soft fingertips of the motel clerk who had almost become his lover only hours before.

His mind filled with the image of Ryan sprawled naked on the bed, hand held out to him. He'd faltered, overthought it.

It doesn't have to mean anything.

Ryan's words came back to him in a flash. It didn't have to mean anything, but it would. It would mean so much more than the younger man realized. In the light of day, he knew it would change everything for him. He also knew that next time – soon – he wouldn't hold back. He wanted Ryan, wanted all of him, and though he knew it definitely meant something, he also knew that he was ready.

Behind him, Ryan stirred and shifted on the bed, instinctually moving closer to him. He felt warm exhalation on his back and then the gentlest kiss between his shoulder blades.

He smiled.

"You awake?"

"Hm?"

"Thought so."

Lane rolled over so he could face Ryan. The younger man's eyes opened drowsily, and a sleepy smile spread across his face. His hair stood up in every direction. Lane chuckled.

"How in the hell is your hair such a mess when you basically slept in one position all night?"

"Ugh, you've been gay less than twenty-four hours, and you're already judgy."

He watched Ryan's eyes close, then pop wide open as if startled.

"I'm sorry. I didn't mean to –"

"Hey, ssshh," he said, pulling Ryan closer to him. "It's okay. Really. I mean, I don't know if gay is the right term for me. Doesn't feel right. But the joke was good, and I'm definitely … open."

Ryan relaxed, then sat up, startled at a sudden pounding on the door. Lane was out of bed and on his feet, but he didn't move toward the sound. Neither moved, frozen in place, waiting to see if the pounding would come again. Silence became time, stretching like a rubber band that could and would hurtle them into action.

Lane didn't relax until he felt Ryan's hand on the small of his back.

"It's probably just some kids playing. It used to happen to us at the motel all the time."

"Maybe," Lane responded, "but that didn't sound like kids."

As quickly and quietly as he could, he grabbed his pants from the floor. He pulled them on, then stepped to the door, looking through the peephole. He didn't see anyone, but he couldn't shake the feeling that something wasn't right. He looked back to Ryan, who was pulling his own pants on, and motioned for him to stay where he was. He reached for the door handle to turn the lock, only to discover it was already open.

Lane frowned. He didn't like that one bit. He couldn't be certain, with everything that had happened the night before, that they'd locked the door, but again, it just didn't feel right. He gripped the handle, counted to three, and pulled the door open quickly. He leaned out the door looking in every direction.

No one there.

Then, when he pulled himself back into the room, he saw the envelope taped to the door with *For Lane and Ryan* scrawled across it. His fingers trembled as he removed it from the door and closed it behind him.

"What is it?" Ryan asked from across the room.

Lane shook his head.

"Trouble."

* * *

Dear Lane & Ryan,

You have done the unthinkable! You've surprised us, and we, as a rule, are never surprised. That's how we survive.

We have been up all night trying to fathom how a friend of Mark's and sweet Ryan from the motel could possibly know one another. Nothing about that makes sense. What series of events could have led to you knowing each other? And knowing each other so well that you share a bed to boot.

You looked lovely last night, lying together in bed. It was wholesome, even if you were both naked.

Lane, we have so many questions for and about you!

Are you the friend who stole Mark's girlfriend? Does it somehow heal you to sleep with a man who escaped us? Is Ryan a substitute for Mark? Was his girlfriend a substitute? A go-between? By fucking her, were you fucking him?

And Ryan ... the one that got away.

You don't know how much we've thought of you since our encounter. We almost had you! Then you ran away.

So few have done that, and we've never had the opportunity to ask why.

Did you sense our intentions? Did you somehow know who we are? Do you know how close you came to the last and greatest pleasure of your life?

You might think I'm overselling our talents, but I am not. I still imagine what your final expression would have been and how your blood would have felt on my skin.

Perhaps there is still time to know ....

You see, you're forcing us to break the rules. We can't assume the fact that you are together and in the same town as us is a coincidence. It's honestly unfathomable. So, we must assume we're being hunted.

Well, two can play that game, and my brother and I play it very well.

Consider this a not-so-subtle warning that the tables are officially turned.

*We can't wait to meet you, Lane, and to see you
again, Ryan.*

Best,
Connor and Caleb

* * *

RYAN READ THE letter for the third time as the reality of their
situation slowly settled over him. Lane hadn't stopped pacing
since the first. He couldn't blame him. If there was enough space
in their motel room, he'd probably be doing the same. As it was,
he sat on the bed staring at the words fighting the urge to curl
into the fetal position.

The letter confirmed his worst fear. The twins, *his twins*,
were not only murderers but the very same murderers who killed
Lane's best friend. He suddenly felt sick to his stomach. His
mouth filled with saliva. He jumped and ran for the bathroom,
slamming the door behind him.

The bathroom tile was cold against his knees as he heaved
again and again until he was empty, and bile burned his throat.
When the heaving stopped, he settled onto his ass, leaning back
against the tub/shower.

A soft tap sounded at the door.

"You okay?"

Ryan considered his response.

"I don't know," he said finally.

"Can I come in?"

"Sure."

He didn't consider how bad he must look beneath the harsh
light of the bathroom reflecting on the tiles. He didn't care. The

113

letter felt like a death warrant. His days were numbered. He was going to die.

Stop it! Stop.

A part of his brain he didn't know reared. It felt strong, hard, and Ryan wondered if this was the fight side of his brain. It's no wonder he didn't recognize its voice. He'd rarely heard it.

The door opened slowly. Lane stood there, staring down at him. His expression was sad.

Without speaking, he grabbed one of the rough washcloths from the sink, wet it with warm water, and knelt down in front of Ryan. He gently washed away the drops of sick from his face with one hand while using the other to massage some of the tension from Ryan's neck.

"They were in our room," Ryan whispered.

"What?"

"Last night ... they were in our room."

"No shit."

"But how do they know you knew Mark?"

"I don't know. Does it matter?"

"No, I guess it doesn't. I thought I saw one of them when I went out for food last night."

He expected Lane to be angry, but instead, the man sat down in front of him and took his hand.

"You sure?"

"No, but it looked like them. I was in the Dairy Queen, and he was at the gas station across the road. With all the traffic driving by, I couldn't get a good look at him. I should have told you, but I guess it slipped my mind after –"

"I get it. I probably would have been second-guessing myself, too. You okay to get up?"

"I think so."

Lane stood and helped Ryan to his feet. He was still shaky, but his legs stayed under him. They walked back into the main room and sat down on the bed, cross-legged and facing each other.

"So," Ryan said, "what do we do?"

"I've been thinking about that."

"Thank God," Ryan said. A nervous laugh bubbled up in his throat. "I thought you were just going to pace back and forth until you dug a hole to Australia."

Lane let out a quiet chuckle of his own.

"I considered it, but I don't think we have that kind of time." He drew in a deep breath. "I think I need to go back home. I think if I go, they'll follow me."

"There's an awful lot of I and me in that statement."

"There is," he said. "I can drop you off somewhere, or if you want, I can get you some cash to catch a bus somewhere. I don't think it's a good idea for you to go back to the motel, but you could head over into New Mexico or Colorado, somewhere out of the way. I'll make sure you have my number. We can stay in touch that way."

The words stung and comforted him at the same time.

"If you think I'm leaving you right now, you're stupid."

His tone was flat and not nearly as assertive as he wanted it to be, but Lane heard him. He watched him process.

"Look," Lane started. "I don't want anything to happen to you. I don't want you hurt."

"And you think leaving me alone will stop that? What happens if things go south? What happens if you…get hurt and can't contact me? I'm supposed to just sit and pretend everything's okay while I wait for a phone call that doesn't come? Fuck that. I'm not doing it."

"Ryan, please."

"No way, Lane. We're in this together. That's how it's going to be. You want to go home? Fine. We'll have a nice long drive, so you can tell me all the reasons you think I'm an idiot for tagging along."

Lane scrubbed his face with his hands and drew in a deep breath. Ryan could tell his was counting to ten, and he prepared to argue until the man gave in. When Lane finally looked at him, he just shrugged.

"Okay, but I don't think it's a good idea."

"I don't either, but we don't have many options."

Lane leaned forward until his forehead touched Ryan's. They sat there in silence for a long time, balancing each other.

"Why home?" Ryan asked after a while.

"Hm? Well, a part of me hopes if they are following us, they'll get bored somewhere along the way. I don't think that'll happen, but a guy can dream. Mostly, I just don't want to do things on their terms. I have a feeling they're not accustomed to returning to the scene of the crime, so to speak. I own Mark's house now. He left it to me in his will, the sonofabitch. I'm hoping it'll make them nervous, but at the very least, I'll have the home field advantage."

"How far away is home?"

"If we leave in the next hour, we could be there by ten tonight."

Ryan considered for a moment, then nodded his head.

"Can I take a shower first?"

"Sure. I need one, too."

Ryan grinned and raised an eyebrow.

"We can save time and shower together if you want."

Lane returned the smile and nodded.

"I like the way you think."

FOURTEEN

WE TURNED IN OUR KEYS IN THE MIDDLE OF THE NIGHT AND WATCH AS THEY DO THE SAME THIS MORNING. THEY GET INTO LANE'S TRUCK AND PULL OUT OF THE PARKING LOT. I WAIT FOR MAYBE THIRTY SECONDS BEFORE DOING THE SAME.

MY STOMACH IS IN KNOTS. I SIT NEXT TO CONNOR, MY HAND GRIPPING HIS THIGH.

THERE ARE A LOT OF PEOPLE ON THE ROAD THIS MORNING. IT'S EASY TO HIDE, TO STALK. WE KNOW THEY'LL BE ON HIGH ALERT, BUT WE ALSO KNOW THEY DON'T KNOW WHAT WE DRIVE. IN MY MIND'S EYE, I CAN ALMOST SEE RYAN LOOKING IN THE MIRROR EVERY FEW SECONDS. I CAN TASTE HIS FEAR.

WHO KNEW HUNTING COULD BE THIS EXCITING?

* * *

LANE AND RYAN drove most of the morning and the early part of the afternoon without stopping. Ryan spent most of his time glancing into the sideview mirror and looking at Lane. Their shower had been, for the most part, a chaste affair. A few kisses as they scrubbed each other down with the tiny, cheap soap every motel in the country stocked. Even with the morning's revelations, Ryan wished there had been time for more, though he was ready.

In the middle of the night, he'd woken up to the comfort of the other man's warmth pressed against him. He'd tightened his embrace, pulling himself closer and listening to him breathe. He felt safe, and despite the way things had gone, he felt wanted – needed. He didn't know what exactly they might end up being, but before he fell asleep, he decided he was all in.

Now, they were driving far too fast down Texas highways, heading for a home that wasn't his.

By two in the afternoon, he had a headache. The sunlight was too bright, and his stomach flipped. He never finished his burger from the night before. He needed food, but he didn't want to bring it up. Instead, he looked out the window and absently rubbed his stomach.

"Hungry?"

Lane's voice was tense but also concerned. "I'm fine."

"I'm not. I didn't really get to eat last night. We're getting low on gas, too."

Lane asked, "You think it's safe to stop?"

"Maybe? If they're back there, I don't think they'll do anything in public."

They rode on in silence until they saw a road sign pointing to the next town.

"I tell you what," Lane said. "I'll drop you off somewhere to order food. While you're getting that squared away, I'll hit up a gas station, get the truck filled up, and then swing back to get you."

Ryan mulled the plan over in his mind and nodded. After crossing the city limits, Lane stopped at a Whataburger, its parking lot almost empty in the quiet hours of a hot afternoon.

But before Lane left the truck, he grabbed Ryan's hand and squeezed it. Ryan smiled in reply and slipped out of the truck, to trot inside.

He ordered two burgers and two orders of fries with sodas. He made sure to order lettuce, pickles, and ketchup only on Lane's burger and was happy he'd made a mental note the night before. They handed him a little plastic number forty-nine, and he slid into a booth to wait. Outside the staff behind the counter, and a tired-looking older woman who rearranged the fried onions on her patty, the place looked deserted.

He tried and failed not to fidget. He was tapping his fingers on the table when someone slid into the booth in front of him. His heart stopped to find one of the twins sitting there.

"HI, RYAN. LONG TIME, NO SEE."

Ice filled his veins. His eyes darted around the room. There was only one exit. His mind raced until a pair of snapped fingers in front of his nose drew him back to the moment.

"What do you want?"

"JUST TO TALK."

"Which one are you?"

The twin smiled. "ISN'T IT OBVIOUS? I'M CALEB."

"Where's Connor?"

"KEEPING TRACK OF LANE."

There was something about the way Caleb said Lane's name. Ryan blushed as if he'd done something wrong.

"HE'S SO HANDSOME. HOW DID YOU TWO MEET?"

Ryan sighed. He knew he was being toyed with, but the only way to find out more was to play the game.

"The same way I met you."

"OH, YOU FOLLOWED HIM BACK TO HIS ROOM FOR A LITTLE LATE NIGHT —"

"It wasn't like that. He … checked in at the motel. He saw a drawing I'd done of you two and thought you might be the same twins who …."

"KILLED MARK?"

Ryan nodded, struggled to find words.

"I told him I'd come with him to look for you. I didn't think it was actually you, though. I don't know why, but I just couldn't make that leap in my head."

"MAYBE IT WAS BECAUSE YOU DIDN'T WANT TO THINK THAT'S WHAT WE PLANNED TO DO TO YOU?"

Ryan shuddered. "Yeah."

Caleb sat back in the booth, looking around the room as if he was bored by the conversation. Then Ryan realized he was waiting for him to ask.

"So, were you?"

"HM?"

The bastard was going to make him say it.

"Were you planning on … killing me?"

Caleb leaned across the table and put his hand over Ryan's. The touch was warm, soft, exactly the way he'd remembered it. The twin looked him in the eyes without flinching. "YES."

"Why?"

"IT'S ALL WE'LL EVER THINK OF DOING. UNTIL WE RETIRE." Caleb's laugh grew ugly. "WAIT, YOU'RE WONDERING WHY WE *PICKED* YOU?"

Ryan nodded, hoping that Lane would come walking into the Whataburger, see Caleb and rescue him.

Caleb slid from the booth and walked around to sit next to Ryan, crowding him close the wall before slipping a hand between Ryan's legs, cupping his cock and balls through the jeans.

"DO YOU REMEMBER BEING IN YOUR MOTHER'S WOMB? NO? WELL, WE DO. WE MISS THAT CLOSENESS." Caleb began moving his palms in slow circles, expertly massaging Ryan whose body betrayed him, hardening under his touch even as his stomach turned in response. "WE TRIED EVERYTHING TO GET THAT FEELING BACK. AS KIDS, WE'D SNUGGLE BARE-ASSED IN THE SAME BED. BUT IT WASN'T THE SAME. BEING APART WAS MADDENING, LIKE AN ITCH THAT YOU COULDN'T EVER REACH. AND THE MORE OUR PARENTS OR THE TEACHERS OR THE SHRINKS TRIED TO DIVIDE US — AND THE FUCKERS DID TRY — THE MORE WE CRAVED THAT CLOSENESS. WE WOULD STICK OURSELVES WITH PINS FROM OUR MOTHER'S SEWING BOX AND PRESS FINGERS OR LIPS TO THE BLOODY SPOTS LIKE BLOOD BROTHERS ARE SUPPOSED TO."

Ryan's dick was at full mast as Caleb squeezed and massaged it. The denim was rough against the dickhead. It hurt in the best of ways. The way his body defied his fear with lust made him want to scream in anger. How could a person feel those two things at the same time?

He should try to escape. But he felt overwhelmed by Caleb's presence.

"JUST AFTER WE TURNED THIRTEEN, CAME BARRY. A FEW YEARS OLDER THAN US, FIT BUT OH SO STUPID. HE FOLLOWED US AROUND, VIED FOR OUR FRIENDSHIP. HE WAS OURS BEFORE WE WANTED HIM.

"SUMMER BREAK. HE FOLLOWED US INTO THE BACKYARD AND BEYOND, INTO THE WOODS THAT LINED THE BACK OF THE PROPERTY. THERE WAS A NATURAL POND OUT THERE, AND WE DECIDED TO GO SKINNY-DIPPING, 'CAUSE WE BOTH WANTED TO SEE WHAT BARRY KEPT HIDDEN BENEATH HIS CLOTHES. GOD I CAN STILL REMEMBER TAKING HIM ALL IN WHEN HE SHUCKED HIS CLOTHES. THAT TAN

SKIN AND THE DARK TUFT OF HAIR UNDER EACH OF HIS ARMS, ABOVE HIS FAT COCK. SO FUCKING SEXY."

Ryan knew if he glanced down he'd see a growing wet spot on his jeans. The head was slick with precum which somehow made Caleb's movements more excruciating and more exciting at the same time.

"IT WASN'T LONG BEFORE SWIMMING TURNED TO ROUGHHOUSING. WE SPLASHED AND DUNKED AND FINALLY ENDED UP IN AN AWKWARD TANGLE OF ARMS AND LEGS IN THE CENTER OF THE POND. I THREW MY ARM OVER HIS SHOULDER, AND HE TURNED HIS NOSE INTO IT.

"'GOSH, YOU SMELL GOOD. IS THAT SOME KINDA BODY SPRAY?'" Caleb's mock little-boy husky voice sent a cold shiver down Ryan's spine, and as if it had been an offer or command, he turned his nose toward Caleb. Inhaled deeply near his armpit. He was musky like any man without deodorant in the Texas heat. But there was something more, something else beneath it that was undeniably attractive.

Stop it…stop it right now. This man wants to kill you and Lane. Stop it!

"I TOLD HIM NO. THAT'S JUST HOW WE SMELL. HE SNIFFED HARD AGAIN AND GRINNED. HE LIKED IT. CONNOR LIFTED HIS ARM, PLACING AN ELBOW ON BARRY'S SHOULDER. HE BREATHED DEEP. I COULD FEEL HIM STIFFENING AGAINST MY LEG. HE SQUEEZED MY ASS WITH HIS FREE HAND.

"CONNOR SHIFTED AND JERKED BARRY'S MOUTH UP TO KISS HIM. SUNLIGHT SET WATER DROPLETS ON FIRE OVER HIS SKIN. I'LL NEVER FORGET THAT. WHEN CONNOR BROKE THE KISS, I PULLED BARRY'S MOUTH TO MINE. SHARE AND SHARE ALIKE, YOU KNOW? WE PRESSED OUR BODIES TOGETHER, A MESS OF STIFFENED COCKS

AND TENSED THIGHS. MOANING INTO EACH OTHER'S MOUTHS. TASTING, TEASING."

A young lady with an angry-red wound around her nose brought over Ryan's food in to-go bags. Connor moved just so, blocking her view of his hand on Ryan's crotch, squeezing so that Ryan nearly coughed.

"WHAT HAPPENED TO YOU?" he asked, tapping the side of his nose.

"My boyfriend didn't like me having a piercing so he ...." Her gesture made what happened clear.

Caleb chuckled. "MAYBE YOU SHOULD KILL HIM."

"Maybe," she muttered and rolled her eyes with all the passion her tired voice could manage.

Once she was gone, Caleb slid a box of fries from the bag to Ryan.

"EAT. I'LL FINISH.

"THE POND. CONNOR AND I SHOT AT THE SAME TIME. THAT WAS THE FIRST STEP ... BACK TO THAT SHARED CLOSENESS OF THE WOMB. WHEN BARRY WENT LIMP ... BETWEEN US, BREATHING HEAVY, LOOKIN' UP AT THE SUN SKY ... I MET CONNOR'S EYES. WITHOUT A WORD, WE PUSHED HIM UNDER THE WATER."

Ryan groaned as fresh semen exploded in his pants. He blushed, looking down, not wanting anyone to see the flush of skin or hear him whimper.

Caleb took one of Ryan's fries. "It takes longer to drown someone than they make it look in the movies. He fought so hard. Maybe he thought it just a game. But we held him down and struggled against him until there weren't any more bubbles floating to the surface. He went limp, again.

"THAT MADE US FEEL WHOLE. IT WASN'T JUST THE KILLING.

WE TRIED THAT WITH SMALL ANIMALS AND THINGS, AND IT DIDN'T UNITE US. NEITHER DID SIXTY-NINING THOUGH YOU'RE MISSING OUT NOT TRYING OUR SPUNK, MY FRIEND. NO, WE NEEDED BOTH THE SEX *AND* THE DEATH TO BRING US THAT PURE BLISS WE HAD BEEN MISSING.

"NOW DON'T YOU FEEL LUCKY? THE MOMENT WE LAID EYES ON YOU, BOTH OF US THOUGHT YOU'D BE PERFECT. SO LOST AND LONELY. I COULD TASTE IT. THAT'S IMPORTANT. IT'S THE BROKEN ONES THAT WORK BEST FOR US. CONNOR AND I CAN FILL THAT VOID INSIDE YOU, AND I DON'T MEAN YOUR ASS."

"Sounds like bullshit." Ryan was shocked by the steadiness of his own voice when his insides felt like a roiling mass of anxiety and guilt.

"MAYBE IT IS," he said, shrugging. "BUT THE MESS ON MY HAND SAYS I'M NOT FAR OFF. SEE, THE THING YOU CAN'T HANDLE, EVEN NOW, IS THAT YOU STILL WANT IT. YOU STILL WANT US. EVEN WHEN YOU KNOW WHAT WE ARE. THAT MAKES YOU EVEN MORE SPECIAL, RYAN."

"We're leaving. Out of state. You don't have to follow us."

"OH, I'M AFRAID WE DO. YOU AND LANE, YOU TWO FINDING EACH OTHER IS ONE THING, BUT ENDING UP IN THE SAME PLACE AS US? THAT'S A SERIOUS CONNECTION. MIGHT EVEN THINK IT BE A LITTLE DIVINE —'"

"A coincidence. That's all."

Caleb stared at him until Ryan had to fight the urge to squirm.

"I WISH I COULD BELIEVE THAT," Caleb said. "BUT IT'S DONE."

Tears threatened to fall, but Ryan blinked them back. He wanted to scream and rage at the perfect face across the table. He wanted to punch him, break his nose, steal his perfection. Maybe then the two would go away, leave him and Lane alone.

"You could try," Caleb said, and for a moment, Ryan thought he'd read his mind. Then Caleb's eyes flicked down to the table, and Ryan realized his hands were clenched into fists. It took concentration, but Ryan finally relaxed them and laid them flat on the table's surface.

"See you around, kid." Caleb got up, winked, then, leaned forward wiping the sticky leftovers of semen onto Ryan's face.

A man with bags under his eyes and a waning mustache walked over to them. He dropped two paper bags on the table. "Gentlemen, we don't permit that kind of behavior at our establishment." He pointed to the door. "Please leave. Now."

"You don't know what you're missing," said Caleb with a smile. He picked up his own bags of take out and strutted out.

Ryan was less steady, but he made it out into the parking lot just moments before Lane arrived. "Got stuck behind a guy filling up five gas jugs and then his pickup." He blinked and read Ryan's face. "What's wrong?" he asked.

Ryan shook his head and climbed into the truck, setting the bags of cold food between them.

"Just drive," he said, and Lane nodded, pulling out of the parking lot and turning east.

FIFTEEN

It was dark when they arrived at the home that had belonged to Mark. Road-weary and emotionally drained, they walked into the house like zombies, dropping their bags inside the door.

"His bed," Lane said, and Ryan nodded.

The mattress and bedclothes had been taken as evidence, and as Lane had been on the road ever since, nothing had been replaced.

"I'm good on the floor," Ryan mumbled, but Lane shook his head.

"The couch pulls out."

With Ryan's help, they threw off the couch cushions and pulled out the bed inside. The sheets were musty, but it was hardly a concern at that moment. For now, they just needed sleep. Both men stripped off their clothes and slipped beneath the top sheet. It was Lane's turn to hold Ryan.

The younger man had been shaken up by his encounter with Caleb earlier in the day, and Lane couldn't blame him. As they settled onto the thin, lumpy mattress, he pulled Ryan into his arms and held him tightly. It was a shock how comfortable and easy it was for him. Ryan's body seemed to fit perfectly against his own. Their legs twined together; their cocks touched. It felt right, natural.

It felt like something good had come from the months of manic loneliness.

He smiled at that and drifted into sleep.

* * *

WE PARK IN THE TREES JUST OUT OF SIGHT OF THE HOUSE. THE NIGHT IS RELATIVELY COOL. WE WATCH THE LIGHTS FLICKER OUT, AND I TURN TO LOOK AT CALEB.

"WELL, THEY'RE HOME."

"YES."

"HOW LONG DO YOU THINK WE SHOULD GIVE THEM?"

"WE'LL KNOW WHEN IT'S RIGHT."

HE'S RIGHT. WE WILL. FOR NOW, WE JUST HAVE TO LIE LOW, WATCH, AND BE READY.

I MOTION TO THE BACK SEAT, AND HE NODS HIS HEAD IN AGREEMENT. WE SLIP BACK INTO THE DARKNESS OF THE CAR AND LIE DOWN FACING EACH OTHER, LEGS INTERTWINED. CONNOR'S HEAD RESTS ON MY SHOULDER. I RUN MY FINGERS THROUGH HIS HAIR AND HUM A TUNELESS SONG. SLEEP COMES QUICKLY.

* * *

"WHAT THE FUCK?!"
     The voice was loud and shrill and had both men scrambling up into a sitting position. Someone else was in the house. A woman stood in the doorway, shadowed by the light blazing through the open door behind her. Her hands are on her hips,

and as her face finally comes into view, Ryan can see she's furious. Beside him, Lane shook his head, trying to clear it. His expression was grim, which only put Ryan on edge.

"Jessica, sit down," he finally said, and recognition flitted at the corner of Ryan's mind.

So, this was her, and he knew all too well what she was thinking.

"I will not."

"Well, I'm not talking to you while looking up at you. Yesterday was a long day. I'm tired and cranky. So, either take a seat or leave."

Ryan was shocked by Lane's tone. He didn't seem angry or even upset. He just sounded exhausted. Jessica, meanwhile, looked like she was ready to throw things, and he shifted on the bed. He wanted her in his sight lines.

"I don't think I will."

"Jessica, please —"

"Please? *Please*?! You've got a hell of a nerve, asshole. When Martha Jean said she saw your truck rolling into town last night, I told her she was mistaken. I told her I'd just talked to you, and you had no intention of coming home anytime soon. You're off on your little mission, and even me telling you I was leaving wasn't enough to change your fucking mind. But I woke up this morning and couldn't shake it, so I drove out here. Not only are you fucking home, but you're sleeping with some man like a goddamned fa —"

Lane was out of bed and across the room like lightning. His entire body was tense. He didn't touch Jessica, but he was so close to her that she instinctively took a step back.

"Say it," he seethed. "You get one time. That's it."

She flinched, but she didn't back away anymore. Ryan admired her backbone. He wasn't sure what he'd do when confronted with that kind of anger.

"I don't even know you anymore."

"That's okay," he said. His voice softened, but only a little. "I'm not sure I know me anymore either. The difference is I've decided that's a good thing. Ryan, this is Jessica. Jessica, that's Ryan. He met the twins and was almost one of their victims. They found out we were traveling together and got the better of us. As far as I know, they followed us from West Texas. They could be anywhere, and you can bet they're planning on killing us the first chance they get."

"What?"

"You heard me."

"Well, you … you gotta call the sheriff."

Lane laughed out loud at that.

"What the hell is he gonna do? We already know what he thinks about men like Mark and Ryan …."

Ryan held his breath on the pullout bed.

"… and me."

If he'd slapped her, Ryan thought, it would have been less of a shock, and the truth was, he was shocked, too. A part of him thought this was all moving too fast. Could Lane really have realized all this in the last few days, or was it just the shock of everything he'd gone through, and that Ryan was with him while it was happening?

Half his brain said it made no sense. The other half told him it was entirely reasonable. He didn't know who to listen to, and he couldn't expend that energy right now.

In any case, Jessica sat down, and Lane seemed to remember

he was naked. Instead of pulling on clothes, though, he crawled back onto the bed and pulled the sheet over him, leaning against the back of the couch next to Ryan.

"Should I —"

"No," he said, squeezing Ryan's hand. "Stay here. I need you here."

Confusion be damned, it felt good to hear that.

"You really found them?" Jessica asked, and Lane nodded his reply. "Well, what are you going to do?"

Lane looked at Ryan and back to Jessica.

"Kill them first if we can."

Jessica fell back in the chair like a deflated balloon. She stared at them both like they were strangers and that perhaps one of them might sprout a second head. She looked around the living room, taking in the entire scene. Her most recent lover was sharing a pullout bed with a man in the home of her former lover, who was killed by two men after sleeping with them in this house.

Nothing in her life had prepared her for this moment. This was the kind of thing that happened to rich, big-city women on soap operas, not in small towns in east Texas with populations of less than ten thousand people. She didn't know what to do, and she certainly had no idea what to say that would change the situation in this house or make it any less confusing.

So, she decided to focus on the immediate issue.

"What can I do to help?"

Lane squeezed Ryan's hand again and leaned forward on the bed.

"Nothing, really. Not here. I don't want you anywhere near Ryan and me, at least not until all this is over."

"Well, I'm not just going to go back to Mama's and pretend like I don't know anything."

"I won't ask you to do that either," Lane said. "Just keep your eyes open. They could be anywhere, but they're going to need supplies. Food, water, all that. If they're smart, and they are, they won't go anywhere together."

"They're tall, and both have thick, wavy black hair and green eyes. They're toned, handsome bastards." Ryan ran a hand across the lower half of his face, as if wiping away a kiss. "And they're charming and cocky as fuck and can talk a person into anything. Maybe that's how they get away with what they do ... over and over again."

Lane nodded in agreement.

"If you hear anything about them, call me. I just want to keep tabs, but Jessica, don't follow them, don't approach, don't do anything that'll get yourself in trouble, okay?"

"I'm not an idiot."

"I didn't say you were."

Jessica huffed, but she stood up and threw her purse over her shoulder. "I've gotta get to work."

"Okay," Lane said with a half-hearted wave.

"Nice to meet you," Ryan said, though his face reddened as soon as the words were out of his mouth.

Jessica froze in the doorway and turned back. She looked like she might say something but decided against it. Instead, she turned away. A moment later, they heard the front door open and close.

* * *

THE BLONDE EMERGES FROM THE HOUSE WITH AN ENTIRELY DIFFERENT ATTITUDE THAN WHEN SHE ENTERED. CALEB AND I WATCH HER WALK TO HER CAR.

SHE'S ALMOST INTROSPECTIVE. SHE GETS TO HER CAR AND LOOKS BACK AT THE HOUSE. I THINK, FOR A MOMENT, SHE MIGHT GO BACK INSIDE.

"I WONDER IF SHE FOUND RYAN AND LANE THE SAME WAY WE DID?"

"PROBABLY," CALEB ANSWERS WITH A SMILE. "LOOKS LIKE IT TOOK THE WIND OUT OF HER."

"YOU THINK SHE'S THE ONE MARK TALKED ABOUT THAT NIGHT? THE ONE HIS BEST FRIEND WAS SLEEPING WITH?"

"I'D PUT MONEY ON IT."

"WHICH MEANS LANE IS THAT FRIEND."

"MOST LIKELY."

"THIS JUST GETS BETTER AND BETTER."

"CALEB?"

"YEAH?"

"I HAVE AN IDEA."

He grins my own grin at me as I start the car and pull away from our vantage point. If we hurry, we can be back in no time at all.

SIXTEEN

It doesn't take long to find the woman. Her car is parked behind a local diner. She must work here but going in together isn't a good idea. We don't know what they talked about in the house. For all we know, they've at least described us to her. There has to be another way. We don't want to wait all day for her shift to end.

We don't want to draw attention to ourselves, either. Kidnapping a woman in broad daylight tends to do that. "If they told her about us, you think they made enough of an impression on her that she'd be afraid?"

"Maybe."

* * *

The diner is precisely what you'd expect it to be. From the checkerboard tiled floor to the brightly colored teal booths, it's like something right out of the 1950s. I walk in alone and look around momentarily before taking a seat.

"I'll be right with you, honey," a voice calls from the far corner. I assume she says that every time the bell over the door rings because she doesn't look at me. She doesn't see me. That's good. I need her to not see me until I'm ready.

I watch her turn in an order, grab a menu, and walk in my direction. She doesn't look up until she's standing in front of me.

"Hello."

SHE STARES AT ME LIKE SHE'S TRYING TO FIGURE OUT A PUZZLE, BUT SHE CAN'T SEE THE PICTURE YET. "Hi, uh…can I get you something to drink to start with?"

"I'LL JUST HAVE WATER."

"Sure, here's your menu. I'll be back in a sec."

AS SOON AS SHE DISAPPEARS FROM VIEW, I WALK INTO THE DINER AND TAKE A SEAT AT THE COUNTER JUST IN FRONT OF THE KITCHEN AREA. SHE STALLS AS SHE WALKS OUT OF THE BACK.

"You decide to change seats?" she asks.

"NOPE, JUST GOT HERE," I SAY. HER EYES DART TO THE CORNER WHERE CALEB IS SITTING. WHEN SHE LOOKS BACK AT ME, I KNOW THEY'VE TOLD HER PART OF THE STORY, IF NOT ALL. THE COLOR DRAINS FROM HER FACE. I HALF EXPECT HER TO RUN, BUT SHE DOESN'T. WITH SHAKING HANDS, SHE WALKS BY ME TO CALEB'S BOOTH.

"Uh, here's your water, hon," she says. "Do you know what you want?"

136

"He does," Connor says from behind her, and she jumps.

"Look," she says. "I don't want any trouble."

"Neither do we," I assure her. "No trouble at all. We just want to talk."

"About what?"

"You know."

The look on her face says she knows exactly what we want to talk about, but she's not quite there yet.

"Honey, I'm the only waitress on duty today. I don't have time for games."

I step a little closer to her.

"If more people made time for games, their lives would be much easier. You want this to be easy, don't you?"

She looks over her shoulder toward the kitchen, weighing her options. She could run. We wouldn't chase her. But she doesn't know that. She's frowning when she looks back.

"You got five minutes," she says.

"Perfect," I say, motioning for her to sit beside the wall.

SHE SIGHS BUT SLIDES INTO THE BOOTH. I SLIDE IN NEXT TO HER AND PUT MY ARM AROUND HER, FLICKING OPEN THE RAZOR SO SHE CAN SEE IT IN HER PERIPHERAL VISION. SHE STIFFENS BUT DOESN'T SAY ANYTHING.

"YOU WENT TO SEE LANE THIS MORNING."

SHE SWALLOWS. NODS.

"HOW WAS HE?"

"What?"

"WHEN YOU SAW HIM? HOW WAS HE?"

"Um, tired, I guess. He had a long drive yesterday."

"YEAH, HE DID. SO DID WE."

"WAS HE ALONE?"

SHE INHALED, THEN EXHALED SLOWLY.

"No."

"HE WAS WITH RYAN?"

SHE SHRUGS.

"I think that was his name. Wasn't all that interested, to be honest."

"Were they in bed together?"

She looks out the window then. In the reflection, we can see the war behind her eyes. She's had the rug pulled out from under her twice in months. First Mark, now Lane. I wish I could read her mind and hear the inner struggle. Instead, I watch her face. Tears are in her eyes when she turns back, but they do not fall. We admire that kind of control. So, few have it.

She nods, then grabs a napkin from the dispenser on the table.

"Were they fucking?"

"Excuse me?"

"Ryan and Lane? Were they fucking? You didn't knock. You just walked in. I just thought you might have caught them in the act."

"No," she says coldly. "They weren't fucking. They were just … sleeping."

"Oh, that's worse," I say. "That's real intimacy. Sleeping with someone is a serious level of trust. That must have been hard to see."

"Yeah. What of it?"

So tough!

"Look, we're not here to hurt or deal with you. We just wanted you to know that we will take care of all this for you."

"What do you mean?"

"We want Ryan, not Lane."

Her brow furrows.

"What do you –"

"Exactly what he said," I tell her. "We're going to take Ryan out of the picture for you."

"I don't understand," she says.

"You don't have to."

"All you have to do is make sure that Lane doesn't come after us when we take Ryan. I know he's attached, but it's new. The bonds aren't nearly as strong as they think they are."

"How do you know that?"

"It's our business to know. It's what we do."

"SO, DO WE HAVE A DEAL?" CONNOR ASKS.

"What makes you think I can keep Lane from coming after you again? I couldn't stop him from leaving before."

"YOU'LL DO IT BECAUSE IT'S IMPORTANT," I TELL HER. "BECAUSE YOU GIVE YOUR WORD."

"AND IF YOU DON'T WHEN WE COME BACK — AND WE WILL — WE'RE ALSO COMING FOR YOU. WE'VE NEVER STUCK AND BLED A WOMAN BEFORE, BUT I ASSURE YOU THAT I'LL DO ANYTHING I HAVE TO DO TO PROTECT MY BROTHER."

"AND I'LL PROTECT HIM."

"SO, I'LL ASK YOU AGAIN. DO WE HAVE A DEAL?"

SHE LOOKS AT ME. REALLY LOOKS AT ME. THEN, SHE LOOKS AT CALEB.

"When will you do it?"

"TOMORROW NIGHT."

"OR THE NEXT."

"WE NEED TIME TO PLAN."

SHE TAKES HER TIME. MULLS OVER WHAT WE'RE SAYING. THEN SHE LOOKS ME IN THE EYES.

"You promise you won't hurt Lane?"

"ON MY BROTHER'S LIFE."

ANOTHER PAUSE.

"Deal."

I SMILE AT HER, AND CONNOR STANDS UP IMMEDIATELY.

"HOPEFULLY, THIS IS THE LAST TIME YOU'LL EVER SEE US," I TELL
HER. "YOU'VE GOT A GOOD HEAD ON YOUR SHOULDERS. YOU
SHOULD GET OUT OF THIS TOWN. IT'S NO GOOD FOR SOMEONE
LIKE YOU."

* * *

RYAN AND LANE spent the morning securing the house. The way
Lane saw it, one way in and one way out, was the safest way
to live now. Luckily for them, Mark had enough hardware and
lumber to barricade three houses.

Every window was boarded by noon, and they'd used two-
by-fours to block the back. Then they'd moved the heavy oak
dresser from Mark's old bedroom in front of the door.

"Just in case," Lane said.

They didn't speak much while they worked. Lane didn't
want distractions, but he could tell something was weighing
on Ryan. So, when they finally took a break after moving the
dresser, he figured it was time to take the lid off whatever was
eating at him.

"What's on your mind?"

"Hmm?"

"You've been quiet ever since Jessica left this morning. What's up?"

"Oh … it's nothing."

"Hey," Lane said, leaning forward. "Don't do that. Just tell me."

Ryan sighed and leaned back against the couch cushions they'd replaced after making up the hide-a-bed. Lane did the same, drawing his foot up under him and turning so he could look the other man in the eye.

"I guess I've been thinking about what you said this morning."

"Which part?"

"You said you already knew what the sheriff thought about men like me and Mark and —"

"And me."

"Yeah. I guess it kind of caught me off guard."

"You wanna know what went through my head right before I said it?"

"Sure."

"That night in the hotel room, you laid it all out for me. I was thinking about what you said about Mark laughing along to gay jokes. You said it made him human but also maybe a bit cowardly. It did. You were right about that."

"I'm really sorry about that."

"Why? It's the truth, isn't it? Being a coward … that's a choice. I don't mean being afraid or shit like that. I'm talking about being a coward. You choose it for yourself or let someone else decide for you, which is as good as making it yourself. Either

143

way, that's on you, even when you choose to protect yourself. We all have cowardly moments. I guess I just decided I wasn't gonna be. Not about this. Not anymore."

"Oh," Ryan said.

Lane watched the younger man process what he said. Ryan didn't look at him. Instead, he stared down at his hands, running his thumbs back and forth over his index finger. Lane wondered if it was a nervous habit. It was the first time he'd noticed it. He could ask, but he decided the time for talking was over.

He leaned forward, took one of Ryan's hands, pulled it to his mouth, and kissed the palm. He kissed it repeatedly until he had Ryan's undivided attention. When he looked up, they locked eyes, and in seconds, he had pulled the younger man onto his lap.

The kiss was rougher than he intended but judging by how Ryan knotted his hands in his hair, Lane figured he didn't mind. It was the kind of kiss that lasts so long that you think you might never come up for air. When their lips broke, Lane pushed the other man's shirt up and over his head. He wrapped his arm around Ryan's waist and kissed the center of his chest, grinning against the flesh at the low moan that escaped the younger man. Lane liked it so much that he drifted to the right until he found the small, pink nub of Ryan's nipple. He sucked it into his mouth, tonguing over it roughly. Lane liked the way it puckered and hardened under his tongue almost as much as he enjoyed Ryan grabbing the back of his head, pulling him tightly to him.

When he thought Lane might explode, Ryan shifted, flipping him onto his back and pressing him into the couch. When their mouths met this time, they lingered, tasting each other, tongues wrestling. Ryan reached around him, pulling at his shirt. Lane pushed himself up, ripped it over his head, and threw it across the room. He was about to fall back into position when the other man touched his chest.

"This is your first time," Ryan said. "Let me."

Lane grinned and rearranged the cushions behind him so he could lie back. By concentrating on Ryan's eyes, his nerves quieted. There was need, desire, and his body trembled, but damn, he hadn't felt safe alone with another guy before then.

Ryan's touches were soft at first. His fingertips ran through the hair on Lane's chest. It tickled, and Lane fought the urge to buck his hips beneath the younger man's touch. His stomach flexed when Ryan leaned down to kiss his stomach, enticed by the warm breath and the velvet lips. The flicker of a tongue made him hiss in surprise, then chuckle when Ryan turned his eyes up to him, feigning innocence.

When Ryan unzipped his pants, he raised his hips and helped push them down. Ryan leaned forward and exhaled. As the warm breath ran down the shaft of Lane's cock, he leaned back against the cushions, covering his face, moaning into his palms. When the younger man ran his tongue from the base up to the tip, he feared he might lose his load before they'd even started. Ryan lingered over the tip, flicking his tongue, kissing, sucking, teasing until Lane groaned loud and long.

He grabbed Ryan by the shoulders, pulling him up, kissing him deep and long, enjoying the bite of his denim jeans against his engorged cock. He needed this man. Needed his arms and mouth. Needed to touch all of him. Lane roughly grabbed at Ryan's jeans, ripping them open and pushing them down until his cock sprang free. He ran his rough hands over the man's ass, squeezing it hard, pulling him up.

"I want to taste you," he rasped into Ryan's ear. "I need a taste."

It was a plea as much as a command, and Ryan smiled, pushing himself up to straddle Lane's chest, bending over him, and bracing his arms on the couch. Lane lapped hungrily at the head when it neared his lips. The head was slick with precum, bitter and salty, and somehow the sexiest thing the man had ever tasted. When Ryan pushed forward, he sucked greedily. What he lacked in experience, he made up for in exuberance. When Ryan started to pull back, Lane gripped his ass and pulled him forward again, appreciating the shock on the younger man's face moments before his head fell back, and he let out a moan.

Lane grunted when he felt Ryan grip his cock. They fell into a rough rhythm, sucking and stroking until the world fell away. For Lane, there was only Ryan, his body, and a growing warmth in the pit of his stomach.

Without warning, Ryan lurched hard, ejaculating hard into Lane's mouth. Lane choked and coughed around the shaft before finding his rhythm once more, swallowing again and again until his own cock went rigid in Ryan's hand and spilled over onto his stomach. After a moment, he let Ryan's cock slip from his mouth.

Ryan gazed down at him, and he stared back.

He mirrored Ryan's smile.

Ryan leaned down to kiss him, then screamed when his head was suddenly ripped back hard. Lane's eyes widened when two identical faces appeared on either side of Ryan's. Connor and Caleb leered at him.

"YOU GUYS PUT ON A HELL OF A SHOW," one of the twins said.

"FUCK YEAH, THEY DO," the other replied.

"I THINK IT'S TIME WE HAD A TALK, THOUGH."

Rage boiled up inside Lane. He tried to push himself up from the couch but found himself weighed down by Ryan, who still sat on top of him. The twins grinned at him. A moment later, everything went dark when one planted a fist in his face.

SEVENTEEN

LANE COULDN'T MOVE. His arms reflexively tightened against restraints at his wrist, and his chest heaved against … rope? He opened his eyes slowly, and as his eyes focused, he realized he was tied to a chair sitting upright. He also realized that he was still naked.

"Lane?"

The voice was quiet, barely a whisper to his right. His head felt heavy as he turned his gaze to Ryan. His recent lover was also naked and bound to a chair. His face was red and swollen. He'd obviously been crying. Forgetting his restraints, Lane attempted to reach for him and was rewarded with mocking chuckles. His head swiveled forward to find the twins standing there.

"NICE OF YOU TO JOIN US."

I GIVE HIM MY BEST SMILE. HE DOESN'T SEEM TO APPRECIATE IT.

"SORRY I HIT YOU SO HARD. I JUST MEANT TO STUN YOU. GUESS I DON'T KNOW MY OWN STRENGTH."

WHEN HE FINALLY FOUND IT, LANE'S VOICE WAS BARELY MORE THAN A HOARSE WHISPER.

"Let him go. You don't want him. I'm the one that's been looking for you."

"WRONG AND WRONG," I reply, still smiling. "WE DO WANT HIM, AND YOU'VE BOTH BEEN LOOKING FOR US. MAYBE FOR DIFFERENT REASONS, BUT THAT DOESN'T CHANGE THE TRUTH OF IT. THE FUNNY THING IS, IF RYAN HADN'T JOINED YOUR LITTLE CRUSADE, HE NEVER WOULD HAVE SEEN US AGAIN. THERE ARE RULES, A CODE OF CONDUCT, SO TO SPEAK. IF A MAN LEAVES US OF HIS OWN FREE WILL BEFORE THE FUN BEGINS, THEN WE DON'T PURSUE."

"BUT IF THAT MAN COMES LOOKING FOR US. WELL, WE FIGURE HE'S FAIR GAME AGAIN. WE MADE THAT NEW ADDENDUM JUST FOR YOU, RYAN. YOU'RE THE FIRST ONE TO SEEK US OUT."

THE SONOFABITCH SOUNDED IMPRESSED, AND LANE'S TEMPER THREATENED TO BOIL OVER.

"AWWW, YOU'RE ANGRY? I WOULD BE, TOO, I GUESS. I MEAN, IF I LED SOMEONE I CARED ABOUT STRAIGHT INTO A TRAP, I'D BE PISSED AS WELL ... AT MYSELF. SO, LET'S JUST MAKE SURE THAT ANGER IS POINTED IN THE RIGHT DIRECTION."

Lane's face reddened. He looked down, away from the twins. He was right, wasn't he? If he'd left Ryan at the motel, he might not be in this mess. And all because of a stupid drawing.

Lane's phone chimed on the coffee table, and he instinctively looked toward it. It was so fucking close, but it might as well be miles away.

The twin on the right picked it up and grinned like he'd been waiting on the text. He walked over to his brother and held it up for him to read. The same grin spread across his face.

"Who is it?" Lane asked.

"THE THIRD PLAYER IN OUR LITTLE GAME."

"IT'S FROM JESSICA. SHE SAYS, 'THEY JUST LEFT HERE. THEY'RE COMING FOR YOU TOMORROW OR THE NEXT DAY. EVERYTHING OKAY OUT THERE?'"

"WELL, THAT'S A LIE. WE WERE THERE HOURS AGO."

"TO BE FAIR, SHE PROBABLY NEEDED TIME TO THINK THINGS OVER."

"LOOKS LIKE SHE MADE UP HER MIND."

"YEAH, BUT WHICH WAY? YOU THINK SHE'LL KEEP UP HER END OF THE BARGAIN?"

"YOU THINK SHE THINKS WE WILL?"

The twins stared at the phone, considering. Ryan strained against the ropes at his wrist, hoping they were distracted enough by the phone to ignore him. His ribs hurt where they'd punched him repeatedly to get him to sit still while they tied him up. His stomach rolled, and for a moment, he thought he might vomit. They'd left him just enough room in the ropes to not cut off the circulation.

But was it enough for him to get free?

They were overconfident. He figured that could be used against them, but how?

"HOW WOULD YOU ANSWER HER?"

Lane looked at his captors with eyes full of revulsion. His face was swollen but no worse than he'd had before. He considered.

"Thanks for the heads up," he said. "We're all right."

The twins stared at him, considering. He guessed they were trying to decipher any hidden meanings. Lane did his best to look innocent. After a moment, the one on the left took the phone and sent back the message.

Seconds later, an answer came.

"All right. Y'all need anything? Should I stop by?"

They looked at him again, those green eyes boring holes into him.

"SHE SHOULD DEFINITELY STOP BY," I tell him, and after a moment, he seems to understand.

"Tell her …. 'Yeah, could you bring us some food from the diner? A couple of chicken fried steaks with brown gravy would do the trick.'"

Lefty looked at him like he was suspicious. He should be. If they sent the message, he thought she might stay away.

The order was Mark's favorite. She used to give him grief all the time for it.

"WHO EATS CHICKEN FRIED STEAK WITH BROWN GRAVY?
YOU'RE A FREAKIN' WEIRDO, YOU KNOW THAT?"

Righty chewed the inside of his lip for a minute, then
nodded. He fired off the message, and again they waited. Thirty
seconds later.

DING!

"'SURE THING. BE THERE IN ABOUT A HALF HOUR.'"

"WELL, THAT'S THAT, THEN. WE SHOULD GET ANOTHER
CHAIR."

"You don't have to do this. You could leave her out of it."

"WE DID LEAVE HER OUT OF IT. YOU BROUGHT HER INTO IT.
YOU SPILLED THE BEANS."

"SO MUCH OF THIS IS YOUR FAULT, YOU KNOW. YOU BROUGHT
RYAN WITH YOU. YOU TOLD JESSICA YOU'D FOUND US AND THAT
WE WERE ON OUR WAY TO FIND YOU."

Ryan watched Lane's head fall forward. He wanted to hug
him, protect him, but he couldn't get free of those goddamned
knots.

"That's bullshit," he whispered instead. "I don't give a shit
about this. I-I'm glad you found me. I'm glad I met you. I'm –"

Ryan looked up at the twins. They considered him with
their heads cocked to either side.

"WHAT?"

"ARE YOU REALLY?"

"Yes, I am," Ryan hissed at him, and he realized it wasn't just words. He was. Life at that motel hadn't been easy. Life on the road hadn't been much easier. But what had happened in the last day and a half? He figured that made up for a shit-ton.

Lane was the first guy he'd slept with that felt like more than just fucking.

Most of his sex life had taken place in shady motels or dimly lit homes with men who did their best to hide who they were. There'd never been much of a connection. They were a means to an end. Lane wasn't like that.

He wasn't so stupid to think he'd fallen in love with the man in the short time they'd been together, but it was more than scratching an itch. This *meant* something, and he intended to live long enough to find out what that something was.

The twin on the left grinned a mocking grin at him.

"Which one are you?" Ryan asked.

The mocking grin never left his face, but he stepped closer to Ryan and leaned down condescendingly to look him in the eye.

"I'M CONNOR," he purred.

With a speed that surprised even him, Ryan's forehead flashed forward, bashing the twin in the nose. A shock of pain ran through his own head, but he was rewarded with a yelp of pain from the twin, who covered his nose as he fell backward onto his ass. Blood ran from beneath his palm as Caleb swooped in to examine his brother.

CALEB'S VOICE WAS SHRILL, "YOU BROKE HIS NOSE!"

Ryan smiled at him. "Good. Now I can tell you two apart."

Caleb lunged at him but fell short when Connor grabbed him from behind.

"LEAVE HIM BE."

"HE. BROKE. YOUR. FUCKING. NOSE."

"Yeah, but we'll do worse to him before the night's done."

Caleb seemed to consider that for a moment. Lane watched him sneer. Connor felt like the leader here, but he was sure that Caleb was more dangerous. There was something about him. Something feral.

Lane watched him closely, waiting for the next move. He watched as his face smoothed, the anger and rage replaced by concern as he turned back to Connor.

"WE NEED TO GET SOME ICE ON THAT. YOU CAN BREAK MY NOSE LATER."

"What?" Ryan asked, shocked.

"WE'RE IDENTICAL. WE INTEND TO STAY THAT WAY."

Lane shouldn't have been shocked by their answer, but somehow, he was. It made no damned sense. He wondered if they killed one, would the other just lie down and die, too?

Couldn't hurt to try, he thought and laughed.

"Something funny?"

"Not really," Lane said. "Was just wondering what you two dickheads want."

Caleb was about to answer when they heard a car drive up outside. Lane winced when the car door slammed.

Damn it, damn it, damn it.

The room fell silent as footsteps approached the front door. The twins stood together. Lane held his breath. Beside him, Ryan shifted in his chair.

The front door opened, closed. Jessica stood there. Her purse was thrown over her shoulder, and she held a plastic take-out bag from the diner. She took in the room and shook her head.

"The hell kind of party you boys throwing?"

EIGHTEEN

CALEB MOVED SO fast that Ryan wondered if he was on wheels.

"Get off me," Jessica said when he grabbed her arm roughly, pulling her farther into the room. She teetered but didn't fall over.

"SHUT UP," I TELL HER, MOVING TO HER OTHER SIDE AND GRABBING THE FOOD BAG FROM HER. I OPEN IT UP AND GRAB THE STACK OF NAPKINS, GENTLY PUSHING THEM TO MY NOSE. IT'S BEEN SO LONG SINCE I'VE SEEN MY OWN BLOOD, AND I'M PISSED.

Connor dropped the bag on the floor, and the foam container popped open, spilling gravy all over the floor. The smell of food made Lane's stomach rumble. He couldn't remember the last time they'd eaten. He licked his lips and realized the stubble around his mouth was sticky. He remembered how he'd first choked when Ryan shot his load. He guessed this is where some of that landed.

"HAVE A SEAT, JESSICA. NO SENSE IN STANDING AROUND."

Caleb pushed her toward the couch when she didn't move right away. This time, she did stumble. She fell knees-first onto the furniture, and it took a minute for her to regain her balance. Finally, she sat down, glaring at the twins.

"What happened to your nose?"

"I broke it," Ryan answered before Connor could say anything. Jessica looked at him, and if he wasn't mistaken, he thought she looked impressed.

"Okay, we're all here. Now what?"

"Now what?"

"Now we tie up all the loose ends. We want to be back on the road by tomorrow."

"So, you're just going to kill us?"

Lane seethed when they laughed at him.

"We never *just* kill anyone."

"There's no fun in that."

"No connection."

"Do you remember the story I told you, Ryan? About how it was the sex and the kill that gave us what we needed?"

"Sex lets us draw it out. We don't generally linger in the killing."

"But we've decided to make an exception for you."

"We're even going to let your boyfriend, Lane, here watch."

"AND AFTER WE'VE MADE AN EXAMPLE OUT OF YOU, THEN WE'LL TAKE CARE OF THESE OTHER TWO AND BE ON OUR WAY. IF YOU COOPERATE, WE'LL EVEN MAKE IT NICE AND QUICK FOR THEM."

"What the fuck?" Jessica shouted, standing up. "That wasn't the deal."

CALEB WAS ACROSS THE ROOM LIKE LIGHTNING. HE BACKHANDED HER, KNOCKING HER BACK ONTO THE COUCH. "IF YOU BELIEVED THAT, YOU'RE DUMBER THAN YOU LOOK."

"THE WAY WE FIGURE IT, LANE WAS OUT FOR REVENGE. HE NEEDED TO MAKE WHAT WE DID TO MARK RIGHT."

"WE GET THAT. HELL, WE RESPECT THAT. I'M HONESTLY SURPRISED NO ONE ELSE HAS EVER TRIED BEFORE."

"AND YOU," I SAY, LOOKING AT JESSICA. "YOU'RE JUST TRYING TO KEEP WHAT YOU THINK IS YOURS. WE TOOK MARK OUT OF THE PICTURE, AND LANE LEFT. ALL THOSE CONFUSED EMOTIONS MAKE FOR BAD DECISION-MAKING, BUT THAT'S ONLY HUMAN, RIGHT?"

"BUT RYAN? RYAN'S SPECIAL. HE WAS SO CLOSE TO US. HE WANTED TO BE WITH US. HE VERY NEARLY HAD THE HONOR OF BEING OUR VICTIM, AND THEN HE RAN."

"THAT SHOULD HAVE BEEN THE END OF IT, BUT WHEN HE MET LANE, HE DECIDED TO COME AFTER US. WHY WAS THAT? DID YOU DECIDE KILLING US WOULD MAKE UP FOR THE FACT THAT YOU WERE

A COWARD? THAT YOU RAN FROM THE THING YOU WANTED MORE
THAN ANYTHING? DID YOU REGRET IT?"

Their eyes fell on Ryan then, and he realized they were
waiting for a response.

He looked from one to the other, then to his feet. "Yes,"
he said.

"YES, WHAT?"

"Yes, I was a coward. Yes, I ran. Yes, I wanted to find you
again, but not to be your fucking victim. I didn't even believe
Lane when he first told me about Mark and you. I thought he had
the wrong guys."

"AND WHEN YOU REALIZED HE WASN'T WRONG? YOU STAYED
WITH HIM. WHY?"

Ryan looked at Lane. Lane looked at him. When Ryan
finally spoke, he ignored everyone else. He spoke directly to the
naked man across from him.

"Because I wasn't going to run. I wasn't going to leave him
alone to deal with you. I wasn't going to abandon him when he
might need me. I wanted to be with him. I *still* want to be with
him. More than I've ever wanted to be with anyone. And fuck
you if you think you're going to take that away from me."

No one spoke.

Lane's eyes were wide and staring at him. Jessica sat
shocked on the couch. The twins looked at each other and then
back to him.

Then they laughed. It was bitter and mocking. They moved to either side of him, grabbed the chair he was tied to, and dragged him around to face Lane. Behind his lover, Ryan saw Jessica shift on the couch and move forward just slightly toward Lane's back.

He heard a metallic click next to his ear. In his periphery, a nasty-looking razor glinted.

Ryan braced himself. He ground his teeth together when the razor flashed downward, slicing a thin red line across his stomach. It was just deep enough to bring beads of blood to the surface. He inhaled sharply. It stung like a bitch, but he wasn't about to give them the benefit of showing it.

In front of him, Lane strained against the ropes. His face was red. His veins bulged. Through the stinging pain, Ryan worried he might have a stroke.

"It's all right," he whispered. "I'm going to be fine."

Behind him, Connor chuckled.

"NO, YOU WON'T, BUT THAT'S SWEET, REALLY."

Caleb grabbed Ryan's right nipple, pulling the tight, puckered flesh forward.

"CONNOR, I WANT THIS."

"OF COURSE."

This time, Ryan did scream. The sound filled the room as Connor removed the nipple in one smooth slice. The twins leaned against each other in ecstasy. Caleb licked the blood away from the backside of the flesh before offering Connor a taste.

161

"I think I'm going to be sick," Jessica said, leaning forward, breathing heavily.

The twins paid no attention to her. They were too busy appreciating their handiwork. She took advantage of their distraction and slipped a pocketknife from her purse. She'd gotten a good look at the way the men were tied up. Connor and Caleb used a single rope on each, tying their wrists to the arms of the chair. Between the wrists, the rope was wound tightly around their chests.

She thought, but wasn't sure, if she could cut the rope in the back, Lane might be able to free himself.

He tensed when he felt the chill of the blade next to his skin but quickly realized what was happening. He instantly quieted, dropping his head like he was trying to look away from what the twins were doing to Ryan.

"SHOULD WE TAKE THE OTHER ONE?"

"HMMM, IT WOULD KEEP HIS NICE SYMMETRY."

Lane did not look up when Ryan screamed again. He worked his wrists, straining against the knots. Behind him, Jessica continued sawing at the ropes, and he felt them give only slightly as she made progress.

When he finally glanced up, he observed Connor dipping his fingers in the blood that ran from the wounds on Ryan's chest. In disgust, he watched Connor dab the blood on his neck. Caleb leaned in and licked the blood away, kissing his brother's throat. Connor moaned appreciatively, letting his head fall back.

"Lane?" Ryan whispered.

"Hold on," he whispered back. "Just hold on."

"WHAT THE FUCK ARE YOU DOING?!"

Lane's head snapped up to see Caleb and Connor staring just over his shoulder. They'd spotted Jessica, and he wasn't free yet. He flexed the muscles in his chest, pushing forward as hard as he could as they moved around Ryan toward his ex-girlfriend.

He heard a punch followed by a grunt. In front of him, Ryan's eyes widened. Fear and anger mingled there. He wasn't sure what was happening behind him, but he knew he had to do something.

And it had to be done, now.

Lane let out a guttural scream as he strained forward one last time. To his surprise, he heard a snap behind him, and the rope at his chest loosened to fall around his waist. His wrists were still bound to the chair's armrests.

Behind him, Jessica screamed. In front of him, Ryan's eyes blazed.

Lane couldn't get loose. So, he did the only thing he could do: pushed himself to his feet, then threw himself to the ground as hard he could. Two loud snaps echoed through the living room. One was Lane's wrist. The other was the arm of the chair. Adrenaline pumped through him when he looked up to see the twins moving in his direction. He forced himself up to his knees and, on instinct, flung his wrist still attached to the chair. The furniture flew hard and fast, striking Connor in the knee, knocking him sideways toward Caleb.

Time slowed as a look of shock ran over both their faces. Connor tripped over his own feet as he fell forward. The sound of tearing flesh filled Lane's ears. At first, he wasn't sure what had happened.

"Connor? Connor, no!"

Caleb went to his knees with Connor. He grabbed his brother's head and pulled it back, exposing Jessica's pocketknife now sticking out of the center of Connor's throat.

A gurgling sound erupted from the wound. Blood poured from his mouth and around the blade.

No one moved.

Caleb cradled his twin in his arms, lowering him to the ground.

"Connor? Connor, please. I'm sorry. It wasn't my fault. It was him. Connor, please, don't die. You can't leave me alone."

Connor answered with another gurgling rasp. His body convulsed as he gripped his brother's shoulder.

Lane looked from the twins to Ryan to the floor where Connor's straight razor lay neatly folded in front of him. He pushed himself to his knees, grabbed the blade, and quickly crawled to Ryan, cutting at the rope at his wrist.

Behind him, Caleb sobbed. He didn't seem to care what Lane was doing, but Lane knew that wouldn't last forever. He worked harder at the rope until it finally gave with an audible snap and creak. Wrist freed, Ryan grabbed the razor from him and began working on his other wrist.

Lane's head fell against Ryan's knee. He did his best to control his breathing, but his senses were still running at their highest capacity.

He heard the soft thud of Connor's lifeless body being laid out on the floor. Heard the shuffle of Caleb pushing himself to his feet.

He whirled around to see Caleb staring at him. The lone twin no longer looked human. His face was contorted with rage and loss. He took long, ragged breaths as he crouched in a predatory attack position, curling his hands until they looked like talons.

"Ryan, babe, hurry."

A low growl escaped Caleb's throat, rising to a primal scream as he lunged forward. An explosion from the couch cut off his scream. The side of Caleb's head disappeared in a cloud of gore, and he fell in a heap on the floor.

Ryan and Lane looked in the direction of the sound to find Jessica holding a large revolver in her hand. Her face was bruised and bloody. A gaping wound let flow a river of blood from her cheek. Her hand trembled, and the gun fell to the floor seconds before she collapsed back in a heap onto the couch.

NINETEEN

THE SHERIFF LEANED over the hospital bed. "Tell it to me again."

Lane had a fresh cast on his broken wrist and a few bruises and scrapes, but the doctor insisted he stay overnight "just in case."

That hadn't stopped the Sheriff from bullying his way into the hospital room to question him about the dead men they'd removed from the living room.

"They came into my house and tried to kill me, Jessica, and Ryan. We defended ourselves. What more do you need to know?"

"And who is Ryan, exactly?"

"He's —" Lane stopped. He wasn't entirely sure how to describe Ryan or what to call him. He was in a separate room on this floor with his torso wrapped in bandages. The doctors had stitched up the wounds on his chest and wrapped his bruised ribs, but there wasn't much they could do for either of their real wounds.

He looked up at the Sheriff. "He's important."

Winters glowered at the answer. Lane could feel the unease and the revulsion rolling off the man in waves. Two days ago, that would have mattered. Now he didn't give a shit what this blowhard asshole or anyone else thought.

"Why are you here, Sheriff? This is Texas. They were in

my house. I have a right to defend myself. If this was anyone else under any other circumstances, you'd be slapping them on the back and telling them not to worry about it. Hell, you'd throw them a little party if you thought you could get away with it. So, tell me, is it the gay thing or the fact that I took care of the business you should have cleaned up yourself?"

The man's face turned purple at that. Lane half-expected him to punch him, but he didn't.

"Do me a favor," the Sheriff said finally. "As soon as you're up and moving, get the hell out of my town."

He didn't wait for a reply. He turned on his heel and left the room like the devil was chasing him.

Lane stared at the ceiling for a moment, then decided he couldn't take the quiet. He pushed himself up and out of bed. The hospital floor was cool beneath his bare feet, and the antiseptic smell bordered on overpowering out in the hallway as he made his way down to Ryan's room.

The young man was lying in bed, his eyes closed, bathed in the soft fluorescent lights behind the bed.

Lane pushed a chair beside the bed and sat down to study Ryan's face. There were bruises, but none worse than his own where he'd punched. Those ribs would be hurting like a bitch if it wasn't for the IV that he was sure had something high-powered in it. He fussed at the bedclothes for a moment, straightening them.

"Since when did they hire you as a nurse on this floor?"

Lane looked up to see Ryan staring at him, smiling.

"Well," he answered. "someone's gotta take care of you."

"Is that so?"

"Yeah, you were doing a shitty job of it at that motel."

Ryan's smile widened.

"You looking for a full-time position?"

"I ... yeah, maybe I am," Lane answered. "You ready to take me on?"

"Well, you got a lot to learn, but after your interview this afternoon, I think you might just be right for the job."

He shifted slightly in his bed. Lane couldn't figure out what he was doing at first. Then, it dawned on him that the younger man was trying to make room for him to join him. He did his best to help, rearranging the IV line so he wouldn't crimp it. He settled gingerly next to Ryan, lying down and slipping his arm over the man's waist.

"Jesus Christ," a voice spoke from the doorway, "how many times am I going to walk in on you two in bed together?"

They both looked up to see Jessica standing there, shaking her head.

Lane grinned. "I mean, you're the one that just keeps walking in without knocking."

"At least you've got clothes on this time," she said. "Mostly. Your ass is hanging out the back of your gown."

"You don't have to look."

"I know I don't," she said, "but I am. So there."

Lane grimaced as she stepped into the light. Her face was bruised and swollen, and white bandages covered her cheek. Unlike Ryan and himself, however, she was wearing street clothes.

"They letting you go home?"

"Letting? I told them to give me my shit and the forms. I'm getting out of here tonight. Wanted to check on you two first, though."

"Appreciate it," Ryan said.

"What do you two plan on doing now?"

Ryan didn't turn his head, but his eyes moved to look at Lane.

"We haven't really had time to talk about it," he said.

"The sheriff suggested I find another place to live," Lane added.

"Suggested?"

"Strongly suggested."

She nodded at him and frowned.

"I called up my sister. She's got room at her place in Florida. I think I'm going to go get tropical for a while."

"Sounds like fun," Ryan said.

"Yeah, well, it'll be different, at least."

She opened her mouth, looked from one man to the other, and shook her head. "Y'all take care," she said. "Let me know where you settle."

"Will do," Ryan and Lane answered in sync.

Jessica rolled her eyes and disappeared into the hallway.

"I'm sorry you have to leave your home," Ryan said after a moment. Lane sat up to look down at him.

"I'm not."

"You aren't?"

"Nope. I think a fresh start sounds like exactly what I need."

"Together?" Ryan asked.

"Together," Lane answered, lying back down and snuggling as close as he thought was safe.

"Any ideas where?"

"Nah. We'll decide tomorrow."

Ryan leaned over just far enough to kiss Lane's head. "Tomorrow."

Ryan fell asleep almost as soon as his head hit the pillow. Lane supposed with that many drugs in his system, he might do the same.

But he didn't. All he had were his thoughts, and tonight they were filled with beautiful, evil Caleb and Connor. Twins he'd helped kill. Twins that couldn't bother him or Ryan ever again except in their thoughts ... their dreams.

As if echoing his thoughts, Ryan whimpered in his drug-induced sleep. Lane wondered if, even now, the twins were hunting him in the dark, trying to seduce him to their bed. He leaned forward and kissed Ryan's forehead.

"Sssh," he whispered. "I'm here."

Ryan's whimpers quieted, and Lane smiled, lying back against their shared pillow.

"You killed my boys."

Lane blinked, sat up as quickly as he could without waking Ryan. A woman stood in the doorway of the hospital room. Stood there staring at him, her eyes unreadable.

"What?"

"You killed them," she repeated. "You killed my boys."

Shit.

Lane reached for the nurse call button, but the woman held up a hand, walked closer to the bed. Between her mascara-stained eyes and her quivering lips, he faltered. When she finally reached him, she grabbed his hand before he could pull it away.

"I was just down in the morgue. I had to identify them. You killed them."

There was no use denying it, he supposed.

"Yeah, I did," he said.

She smiled then, somehow sad and relieved all at once.

"Thank you," she whispered, squeezing his hand. "I think, maybe, my nightmares are over."

"I think we might still have ours for a while."

"You've earned them," she said, nodding and looking down at Ryan. She smiled then. Not a sad smile. You might even call it radiant. "But you two will make better dreams together."

Lane tried to speak, wanted to say something, but no words came. In any case, the woman turned and walked from the room, disappearing around the corner like she'd never been there.

Lane looked down at Ryan and exhaled.

He didn't lie back down. He had no intention of sleeping, not tonight anyway. Tonight, he'd watch out for Ryan. Maybe tomorrow night he'd return the favor. Settling back on the bed, he pulled Ryan closer until he was nestled against his chest.

Just in case.

ABOUT THE AUTHOR

W. Dale Jordan is an out and proud gay author living with his husband in the wilds of East Texas. Growing up, his imagination was always just a little too big for him, and it often spilled onto the page. Today, he splits his writing life between fiction and journalism. He is a big believer that representation in media is vital to equity in the real world and incorporates those ideas into his writing, whether it's a scary creature feature or a fantasy tale like those he loved growing up.